Dad,

Hope yo

Christmas '91.

xxxxx + Joel.

Would I lie to you?

Ted Egan is known and loved across Australia as a singer and writer of bush ballads, and has often been dubbed 'the authentic voice of central Australia'. He was born in Melbourne in 1932, and left for Darwin at the age of 16. He worked with the Department of Aboriginal Affairs for the next twenty-five years, in occupations ranging from grave-digger and crocodile-shooter to reserve superintendent, teacher, and Director of Special Projects. In the main he was given postings in the bush, and it was there that he met many of the larger-than-life characters who are now the subjects of his songs, poems and yarns. Since 1975 he has lived in Alice Springs, writing and singing songs, and telling yarns for a living. He has presented his own series on national television and hosts The Ted Egan Outback Show several nights a week in Alice Springs.

Peter Viska's distinctive cartoons have made him one of Australia's best-known and most successful illustrators. Born in Perth in 1946, he spent twelve months of his youth in the far north-west of Western Australia, which gave him firsthand experience of the spirit and characters of the outback. He moved to the eastern seaboard in 1970 and after working as a cartoonist on various newspapers and magazines he turned to book illustration. The enormous success of his first commission, *Far Out Brussel Sprout*, enabled him to set up his own animation company, and he now divides his time between this and book illustration.

TED EGAN

Would I lie to you?

The Goanna Drover
& Other *very* True Stories

Illustrated by PETER VISKA

VIKING O'NEIL

Viking O'Neil
Penguin Books Australia Ltd
487 Maroondah Highway, PO Box 257
Ringwood, Victoria 3134, Australia
Penguin Books Ltd
Harmondsworth, Middlesex, England
Viking Penguin, A Division of Penguin Books USA Inc.
375 Hudson Street, New York, New York 10014, USA
Penguin Books Canada Limited
10 Alcorn Avenue, Toronto, Ontario, Canada M4V 1E4
Penguin Books (N.Z.) Ltd
182–190 Wairau Road, Auckland 10, New Zealand

First published by Penguin Books Australia 1991

10 9 8 7 6 5 4 3 2 1

Produced by Viking O'Neil
56 Claremont Street, South Yarra, Victoria 3141, Australia
A Division of Penguin Books Australia Ltd

Typeset in 11/15 Century O.S. Expanded 10% by Bookset
Printed in Australia by Impact Printing, Brunswick, Victoria

National Library of Australia
Cataloguing-in-Publication data

Egan, Ted.
  Would I lie to you?: the goanna drover and other
  very true stories.

  ISBN 0 670 90460 0.

  1. Tall tales – Northern Territory. I. Title.

A823.3

Contents

Preface

A R THERE MATE, AND G'DAY,
I use with confidence this typically Australian form of greeting, for I feel that if you have purchased or even contemplated buying this book you are a friend for life.

But a word of warning! I have been asked to put together a book of the yarns – oops, true stories – I have been spinning over many years at my show in Alice Springs. At last I have relented, so here are a few for you. I have tried to write the stories in the same manner I relate them. So please excuse the bad grammar and spelling. I done me best.

And I know I'm a publisher's nightmare when it comes to heights, weights, measures and currency. Sometimes it's a Collingwood six-footer, sometimes it's a 'fifty' of flour, occasionally twenty dollars (but never twenty bucks – I'll leave that to the Yanks). Short of a quid seems definitely more impecunious than minus a dollar; and eight stone wringing wet seems a more impressive fighting weight than fifty kilos. I guess we'll always have this dilemma in Australia as long as there's somebody who remembers that the blood was sometimes an inch deep on the floor of the Six Mile Pub at Wyndham, while ever there is the nostalgia that the bloody beer (only) cost four and six in bloody, bloody Darwin.

Cheers!

Ted Egan

The Original E.T.

NOW, first and at all times, I want you to believe that everything you read in this book is true. Absolutely. Would I lie to you?

I'll get stuck straight into things because the Managing Editor had the hide to ask me whether I could meet her publishing deadline. The cheek! I was quick to remind her that in the Northern Territory, where I live, I am known either as E.T. or P.T., standing for either Early Ted or Punctual Ted.

I am an absolute stickler for punctuality. I drive people

crazy with my obsession about getting things done on time. I guess I am a bit like a reformed drinker, prone to stress the point too much, because I haven't always been punctual. In fact, when I was a school kid I was so unpunctual I was almost dyspunctual. But my life changed dramatically one dreadful week.

School started at 9 a.m. on Monday morning, and I arrived for my first lesson at 2.15 p.m. on Tuesday afternoon. I hasten to stress that these were not 'the good old days': oh no, these were the days before most of my readers were born, the 'bad old days'. And I'll never forget our classroom teacher! She had a nose like a pick, and there she was standing at the classroom door, daring me to cross the threshold. I looked, and in her hand was a bloody great lump of four-by-two timber, complete with a big rusty nail sticking out of the end!

'You cross that line, son, and I'll give you the greatest flogging you've ever had,' she warned, 'and furthermore my lad, the headmaster has a new cane and he's going to try it out on you after I've finished.' Smoke was coming out of her ears, so I gulped and I composed myself.

'Teacher,' I stammered, 'I know I'm late, but I have a very valid excuse – I think.'

'You've always got an excuse,' she roared, brandishing the stick. 'What is it this time, pray?'

'I'm late on this occasion, teacher,' I said, 'because my Dad has only one pair of pyjamas.'

She took on a glazed look of disbelief.

'Well,' she acknowledged grudgingly, 'that's a better-than-average start, carry on!'

'That's all there is to it, teacher,' I said. 'That's the total reason for my tardiness.'

She needed detail, I could see, and she still looked threatening, so I quickly continued.

2

'Yes, teacher, Dad has only one pair of pyjamas, and Mum washed them last Sunday, and hung them on the clothes line, thinking that on such a lovely sunny day Dad's pyjamas would dry in time for him to wear them to bed that night . . .' I looked at her. She was sceptical.

'Teacher, you'll recall that we had that thunderstorm on Sunday evening, about five o'clock?' She nodded.

'Well, Dad's pyjamas were still on the line and they got wet, so Dad couldn't wear them to bed. As a result, he had to do something that he'd never done, or even contemplated in his life before.'

I checked her out. She ran her pointy little tongue over her dry lips. 'Dad had to sleep . . . *in the nude!*'

I waited for that to sink in.

'So. There's Dad in bed, *in the nude*, fast asleep. Then, at about midnight, there's a terrible commotion in the fowlhouse in the back yard. My Dad sat bolt upright in bed, listened to the noise, and roared, "It's him!"'

'Then he gave Mum an almighty shake. She woke and said, "What in the hell's going on?"'

'"Listen!" Dad whispered urgently, "It's him!"'

'Mum cocked her ear, and then said, "Oh no, not him!"'

I looked at the teacher. She was confused.

'Teacher,' I explained, 'in our neighbourhood there's a dreadful chap who goes round in the middle of the night stealing people's chooks. He's known either as the Fowl Filcher or the Chook Crook.'

'Go on,' said the teacher. 'So?'

'Well,' I said, 'Dad was certain it was him, because of the lateness of the hour and the direction of the noise, see, but he didn't want to switch on the light, or anything like that. Oh, no. That would disclose that he was up, and alert. So in the darkness, and *in the nude*, my Dad pole-vaulted out of bed and crept over to a cupboard. On the top of the cupboard Dad located, by touch . . . his old double-barrelled shotgun.'

I checked to see how I was going. I was winning!

'Yes, teacher,' I said, 'Dad gently placed the shotgun on the table. On a shelf he located a box of cartridges. He opened the box, extracted two cartridges, then cracked open the shotgun and slammed a cartridge in each barrel. Then, he cocked the shotgun. Both barrels were ready to fire simultaneously! In the darkness, and *in the nude*, Dad crept out of the bedroom onto the side verandah. As he opened the door to the verandah Dad could hear the dreadful commotion in the fowlhouse, full blast. Teacher, as Dad crossed the verandah he signalled to our faithful old dog, Humphrey, to get out of his kennel and lend a hand . . . sorry, a paw. Humphrey sensed the urgency of the moment, teacher, got out of the kennel and, like the faithful retriever he was, started to creep across the back yard at my father's heels. So here's Dad, in the darkness and *in the nude*, clutching his shotgun, fully cocked and ready to fire both barrels simultaneously, crossing the backyard with Humphrey right at his heels. Teacher, Dad didn't want to be seen against the skyline, so he crouched very low as he crossed the yard, and Humphrey's right there at his heels. Then Dad reached the fowlhouse, stopped to open the gate, and suddenly . . . Humphrey's cold, wet nose touched my Dad's dangling appendages! Dad jumped four-foot-six into the air, both barrels of the shotgun went off with an almighty bang, and Teacher, I've been cleaning bloody chooks for the last day and a half!'

The teacher fainted!

So, it's Punctual Ted! OK?

The Goanna Drover

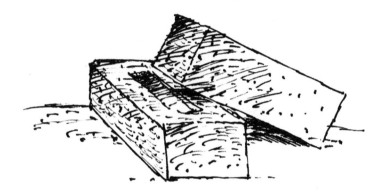

AND NOW, dear reader, I want your opinion, because I respect your intelligence. Honest. You see, I tend to write things on impulse, and because I am such a stickler for the truth myself I naturally assume that everybody I meet is the same. But occasionally I have my doubts.

Take the fellow I met recently at the Birdsville Pub. Well, we had a few drinks together, and talked on a wide range of philosophical topics, as one does at Birdsville. Eventually we came to the subject of droving, so strictly on a conversational level I mentioned my period droving with Tom Burrows. Nothing special, nothing flash, but, yes, I've 'had a go, mate', as Australians tend to say. I've had a go.

Well, back he came, this joker at Birdsville. 'Son, son,' he said to me. (That's the type of bloke he was: he was fifteen years younger than I, and he was calling me 'son' and I was buying the drinks!) 'Son,' he said, 'I am an exceedingly famous drover myself.'

I shouldn't have been surprised, should I? He had already established that he was the middleweight box-ing champion of Birdsville; he was the ballroom-dancing champion also, specialising in the 'cross chassis and lock' – which he had demonstrated by dancing me around the bar: it goes over well at Birdsville among the ringers, I can tell you. And he claimed to be the speed ice-skating champion of Birdsville. So, naturally, when he told me he was a famous drover I believed him, didn't I?

I didn't want to be a knocker, but I had to say to him 'I've never heard of you as a drover'. He immediately chided me, 'Son, son, you wouldn't hear of a bloke like me. You shouldn't expect to. You see, I'm not one of those run-of-the-mill cattle or sheep drovers! Oh, no!' He looked around furtively before he continued. 'No. I'm an under-cover agent. I'm a goanna drover.'

I was so convinced that I wrote this little piece about him but, as I say, now I'm having these nagging doubts. So when you read this little piece I wrote – on impulse – don't concentrate so much on the metaphysical aspects, or the iambic pentameters, or stuff like that. Just let me know whether you reckon he told me a fair dinkum story or not. Address your letters to Ted Egan, Birdsville Pub, Queensland, Australia. Here it is.

I was drinking in the bar of the Birdsville Pub,
When this long, skinny feller came in,
He had greasy old moleskins, concertina leggins,
On his face was a devilish grin.
Well, he breasted the bar,
Gives a little 'Yee-har',
Says, 'I'm sorry that I've got no dough,
But I'll spin you a yarn
If you buy me a beer,
It's a story that you all should know.'

For he said he was a drover,
The finest in the land,
He was travelling around Australia,
Ten thousand goannas in hand.

He said: 'I'm drovin' ten thousand goannas,
Been five years on the track,
Started up at Cairns where we dipped the mob,
Then we headed for the great outback
Went due west to 'the Curry'
Across them black-soil plains,
But we got bogged down at the Isa,
And had to fit the goannas with chains.

Walkin' 'em down the Murranji Track
The goannas started climbing trees,
But a drover's got to improvise,
And I solved the problem with ease.
The monsoon rains were due to start,
There was no time to lose,
So I got forty thousand sardine tins,
And fitted the goannas with shoes.

We clanked across them gibber plains,
She's hard on shoes out there,
But the move paid off in the Channel Country,
'Cos the rivers had filled Lake Eyre.
I got an old bull camel,
Showed him who was boss,
I hit the camel with the old 'brick trick'
And he water-skied the goannas across!

So, here I am at the Birdsville Pub,
And if you buy me another drink,
I'll tell you about me future plans,
That's fair enough, wouldn't you think?
He said, 'I'll have a rum this time,
A double! Good luck! Yes, Cheers!
Well, I'm off now mates, so long, Hooroo!
I'll be in Hobart within two years.'

We called, 'Hang on a minute!
We can see you're a bit of a star,
But droving goannas to Tassie, mate,
That's taking things a bit too far.
How would you get them goannas
Right across Bass Strait?'
He flashed us all his devilish grin
And said, 'I'm not goin' that way, mate!'

But he said he was a drover
Finest in the land
He was travellin' around Australia,
Ten thousand goannas in hand!

So let me know what you think. Incidentally, do you know what we call goannas around Alice Springs? We call them 'overland trout'. And you all know about the 'brick trick', of course? Good. I need to check, because I get strange looks from people like Japanese tourists in Alice Springs when I talk about it. It seems to lose something in the translation – even when I explain about 'keeping your thumbs out of the way', they still don't seem to get it.

Willow on Leather: Bush-style

INHERITED from my dear old Dad a great love of the wonderful game called cricket. When I was a kid my Dad used to take me along to the MCG, and one of my boasts is that I've seen the greatest batsman who ever played, Don Bradman, and the greatest bowler of all time, Bill 'Tiger' O'Reilly. In fact I wrote a song about them called 'The Tiger and the Don'.

My Dad said 'Feast your eyes upon
The Tiger and the Don

You'll never see a pair like them again.
Don's the greatest bat of all
And when The Tiger's got the ball
He puts the fear of God in all those Englishmen . . .

My Dad was very knowledgeable about cricket, and had a delightful fund of stories. One I liked concerned the very unpopular English captain Douglas Jardine. Jardine was an aloof turd of a bloke, it seems, and particularly disliked Australians, whom he felt to be an inferior colonial species. Jardine was what was called a 'Gentleman' player, being an amateur, and the professional players for England were called 'Players'. The two different types of cricketer used to enter the playing field through different gates, and the Players had to call the Gentlemen 'mister'. Imagine what a pay the Australians gave them over that! Once during the 1932 Bodyline tour the Poms were playing South Australia, and the wicketkeeper for England, Les Ames, took a catch behind the stumps.

'Nice catch, Ames,' said the patrician Jardine.

'Thanks, Mr Jardine,' replied Ames, dutifully.

The Australians took this on board. When Jardine was batting the South Australian fast bowler, Scott, caught an outside edge. The South Australian wicketkeeper, Hack, gleefully accepted the snick.

'Howzat?' Up went the umpire's finger.

'Nice catch, Hack,' called Scott.

'Thanks, Mr Scott,' responded a tongue-in-cheek Hack.

Apparently Jardine was singularly unimpressed. In the next Ashes series he said that he 'neither desired nor intended to play against the Australians'. Thanks Mr Jardine.

On another occasion in Sydney Jardine was batting, and the flies were particularly troublesome. Impatiently, Jardine was attempting to keep them away from his face. His arms flailed in between deliveries. From the boundary came the bellowing voice of the mighty 'Yabba', the greatest barracker the game has known.

'Leave our flies alone, you Pommy bastard!' he roared.

Cricket is immensely popular in the bush, and there is an incredible level of knowledge about the game. Lots of bush people sit up through the night to listen to the cricket over the radio. Nowadays there's even TV coverage from overseas.

Once I was in the stock camp at Mt Denison station, and Norman Hagan and I were sitting on our swags by a portable radio, listening to the cricket out under the stars, having a pannikin of rum, and generally enjoying life. We had a wonderful old Aboriginal bloke named Coniston Johnny with us in the camp. He couldn't sleep, so he got out of his swag and joined us by the fire. Australia was playing England at Manchester, and Alan Davidson was getting stuck into the English bowlers. 'Davo' hit a six, and Norman roared, 'Good on you, Davo'.

Old Johnny was suitably mystified. 'What's going on?' he asked.

'Oh, we're listening to the cricket, and Davidson just hit a six.'

Johnny knew about the game of cricket for he had often watched us having a game at the station. 'By Jesus, Norman,' he said, 'if he's hitting them around now, what will he be like when the sun comes up and he can see the ball properly!'

At Kalkeringi, or Wave Hill, they have a cricket club. It was originated by a mighty bloke named Frank Dalton, who was running a little grog shanty which he called Frank's Bar and Grill. Peter Young, a police inspector from Darwin, told Frank that there were two alternatives: get legal, or get knocked off. So Frank opted for legality and got a club licence to serve grog to members of the Wave Hill Cricket Club. Frank built the Frank Dalton Memorial Grandstand (a bough shed), poured a concrete pitch, made some cardboard seagulls which he places out near the boundary when a match is played, and erected a barbed-wire players' race through which the batsmen have to enter and leave the ground. Understandably they have to conduct a few games each year to justify the licence, and the doughty Wave Hillites take on such cricketing greats as the Katherine River Rats and the Manbulloo Marauders. It is compulsory to have a substantial wager on the game, and Frank's decree is 'All bets in cartons (of beer, of course)'.

A couple of years back a team of army blokes were working in the bush around Wave Hill, so Frank saw the opportunity for a game – and the mandatory side wager.

'You chaps play cricket?' Frank asked disingenuously.

'Yes,' said the army boys.

A game was quickly arranged with a side wager of a friendly twenty cartons of beer – and at $25 a carton that was a sizeable bet. Frank suggested that they come down early on the Saturday morning, at about eight-thirty, for a pre-match breakfast: bacon and eggs and 'a few phlegm-cutters'. Down they came, and Frank started pumping the Bundy Rum into them. By 11 a.m. they were legless, whereas Frank's players, all seasoned hands on the rum, had been taking it easy. So the W.H.C.C. duly thrashed the army team, the side bet was collected and the army boys left the area the following week. The locals' mirth was unbounded.

About twelve months later another army survey team arrived in the area. Frank was delighted.

'You boys play cricket by any chance?'

'Yes. Is there a chance of a match out here?'

Was there ever? This time Frank suggested a wager of thirty cartons, and the army boys accepted. A pre-match breakfast? Great. They rolled up at eight-thirty and got stuck right into the bacon and eggs, washing it down with great tumblers of rum. Frank could hardly contain himself, and at 11 a.m. he declared that it was time for the game to commence.

Suddenly there was the unmistakable sound of helicopters. Frank raced out into the open, looked up, and there they were: four choppers, coming in from north, south, east and west, and bringing in – the army cricket team, sober, athletic, in their flannels, ready for *action*! The Wave Hill boys were butchered, but you've got to hand it to Frank Dalton. He took it in good part, put on a big barbecue at Frank's Bar and Grill, and proceeded to back Collingwood for the 1990 AFL Premiership at odds of ten to one – all bets in cartons, of course.

You see some great cricketing talent in the bush, fellows who could have played in the bigger leagues if they'd moved to the cities, but I've never seen a talent to match that of Wayne Kraft, and I've seen the greatest players, remember.

Yes, Wayne Kraft. What a batsman. I was the captain of a team in the Alice Springs cricket competition a few years

back, and we did very well. We were mainly older chaps and the reason for our success, I think, was that we were very relaxed about things. We used to have a keg of beer at the game, and this helped us to develop the level of serenity required to see us through a match. Krafty – as he is called – always came along to watch us, but he never played. He was content just to stand around the keg, drinking the odd schooner, and enjoying the cricket that we played. I often asked him to sign up with the team, but his reply was always the same:

'No, sorry Ted, I have played a bit of cricket, but I wouldn't sign up for a team. I'm just too unreliable.'

'How do you mean?' I asked, the first time around.

'Well,' was his considered response, 'I have been known to turn up an hour late for a game. And that wouldn't suit you – Early Ted – would it now?'

'It certainly wouldn't,' was my quick reaction.

And then to everybody's surprise we got into the finals. One-day matches, of course, and here we were in the preliminary final with the loser to drop out of the competition.

On the day of the game we were one player short. And there was Krafty in his usual spot, standing by the keg, schooner in hand.

'Wayne, old mate,' I said to him, 'you're in the team today. We're one short, That OK?

'Oh, yes, that's fine, Ted. I don't mind filling in for you. It's just that I wouldn't sign up on a regular basis. You know, the unpunctual factor – an hour late, all that sort of stuff.'

'Right,' I said to him. 'I won't expect anything spectacular from you. You can field out on the square-leg boundary, and bat at number eleven. Just make up the numbers.'

'Good, thanks Ted,' he said, finished his beer, and joined us.

I lost the toss. The opposition batted and they made 184, a reasonable total. We went in to bat, and talk about a collapse: we were nine wickets down for 97 runs, and I walked over to Krafty, who was putting on the pads.

'It's a lost cause I think, mate, but go out, shut your eyes, have a swing, do anything you like. And then we can come back, finish the keg and generally drown our sorrows and think of next season.'

Out walked Krafty, shaped up to bat right-handed, and took block. Two centres, thank you umpire. He took a look around the field, and then . . . Well, it could have been Bradman. He was magnificent. He danced down the pitch and smacked their slow bowlers all round the ground. They put the quicks back on and he hooked, pulled and cut like the Master himself. Cover drives, I've never seen better. A couple of his late cuts were so late they were almost posthumous. And all the time he was farming the strike, just as the Don used to do, keeping the other batsman away from the bowlers.

Krafty finished up with 88 not out, and we won. We celebrated into the night, and all the time I'm looking hard at this mate of many years, this cricketing genius unfurled only today.

'Krafty,' I said. 'Krafty, what in the hell is going on?'

'Well,' he replied modestly. 'I did tell you I'd played before. It's just the punctuality bit that prevents me from playing on a regular basis. Now, come on Ted, be honest, you wouldn't stand for me arriving an hour late for a match, would you?'

'No, I wouldn't,' I grudgingly acknowledged, 'but there must be some way around that sort of trifle. Anyway, that's something to worry about next season. But how about next week. Will you come and play for us in the Grand Final?'

'I'll see what I can do, Ted,' he replied. 'Can't promise anything though. I might be there. I might be an hour late. Who knows?' He was there. I arrived for the big game, and there was Krafty, standing by the keg, lowering his fifth schooner. I went straight to the selectors.

'Listen chaps,' I said urgently. 'Krafty's here, and I want him in the team. And not just at number eleven. No, I want to bat him first drop, number three. This fellow is the goods.'

The selectors respected my judgement, and Krafty was in the side. Again I lost the toss, the opposition batted, and they made 227. Hard to beat. And we lost a wicket in the first over: one for 3. I walked over to Krafty, who was very relaxed, padded up.

'This is it, Wayne. The big one.' He nodded, and I continued. 'Don't do anything rash. Have a look at them for a couple of overs, and then, four an over, lots of singles. See what you can do.' Out he walked, took a look around and took block. Middle and leg, thanks ump. But . . . he was taking block left-handed! What in the hell was going on? Had he gone mad?

I want you to think of the great left-handers you've ever seen, dear reader. I won't take you back as far as Clem Hill, but reflect on the talents of . . . Arthur Morris, Neil Harvey, Sir Garfield Sobers, Bill Lawry, Alan Border, David Gower. Think about all of those greats, roll them into one magnificent left-handed package, and you'll have some idea of what we witnessed on that wonderful day in the Alice. He was superb. Square drives as only left-handers in the upper echelons can hit them. Hooks, pulls, cuts, every shot in the book. He was merciless, finished up with 152 not out, and we were premiers. We carried him from the field on our shoulders, drank his health in schooners, and celebrated all night. The MacDonnell Ranges rang with the echoes of classic songs like 'The Bloody Good Drinkers' and 'The Barrow Boys are on the Piss Again'.

During the night, in a quieter moment, I walked over to Wayne and said, 'Mate, you were wonderful. Such talent.'

He looked a bit embarrassed. 'Oh, I look on it as just another innings, Ted. Remember, I did say I'd played a bit of cricket. It's just that . . .'

I finished the sentence for him. 'Just that you're not very punctual. Yes, I got that.'

'Ted,' he confided, 'you wouldn't know how many times I've arrived an hour late for a game. It's not good enough.'

'Oh, well, that's not a relevant factor today, mate,' I said. 'You played today, and we won, and you were . . . bloody magnificent. But, there was one thing I wanted to talk about, and that's your batting technique.'

'How do you mean?' asked Wayne.

'Well, your total approach to things. Last week, when you made 88 not out you batted right-handed, and you were superb. Today, you made 152 not out, and it was equally magnificent. And yet you batted left-handed. What's the go? Are you ambidextrous, or what?'

He thought for a moment. 'No, I don't consider myself to be ambidextrous, or anything clever like that. No, it's just that, with cricket, as with everything else in life, I get great inspiration from my lovely wife Barbara. She's the power behind me, Ted.' He reflected for a moment, and then continued. 'You see, Ted, if I am playing cricket, I always get up on the day of the match, and then I look at Barbara, lying in bed. If she's lying on her right side, well, I bat right-handed that day. But if she's on her left side, well, I bat left-handed. That's my cricketing technique, and it seems to work for me.'

I looked at him in awe. 'It certainly does work for you, mate. We're premiers, aren't we? But, hang on,' I said, 'what if Barbara is lying on her back?'

'Ah, Ted,' he said slowly, ruminatively, 'those are the days I come an hour late.'

Overseas Travel

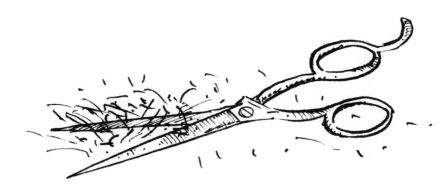

I'M NOT SURPRISED that Tatts Lotto and all the other lotteries are so popular, because a mate of mine not so long ago won $500 000. I won't disclose his name, because he might get plagued with begging letters: I'll call him 'the Fencer'. He's not your 'On guard!' variety, but definitely into barbed wire in a big way. He works mainly out on the big stations east of the Alice.

Well, he won all this money, so he got a bit of financial advice and invested most of it, but the bank manager said 'You might as well shout yourself a holiday as well'. He'd never had a holiday, the old bloke, and he's a lonely old widower with no dependants so he thought 'Why not!'. He went to Maree Kilgariff's travel agency in Todd Mall, and booked the tour he'd always dreamed about – a trip to London, and the continent of Europe. He fixed his passport, and was he excited! He got a stack of new clothes at Bruce Deans' Menswear and he thought 'A man's a bit scruffy for overseas travel, better have a haircut'.

Now I'd better not mention the barber's name either, I'll simply call him 'the Barber', because he's a man not known for his sense of humour. And he's a bit of a wowser, definitely opposed to things like gambling. So in walked the Fencer for his O.S. trim, and the Barber attacked him. Talk about a wet blanket.

'Yes,' said the Barber for openers, 'I heard all about it, so don't bother to bore me with the details of your big win. I just hope you've invested all that money.'

'Well, I've invested most of it,' said the Fencer, 'but I've also booked myself a bit of a holiday overseas.'

'What!' replied the Barber. 'There's no fool like an old fool! Who in their right mind would want to travel over-seas? Where in the hell are you going, for God's sake?'

'Well, I'm off to London first, and then off to the continent of Europe,' said the old chap, a bit peeved at the Barber's knocking attitude. Meanwhile, the haircut was under way.

'London! London!' the Barber sneered. 'You'll hate it. You'll be surrounded by Pommies, it'll piss down with rain all the time you're there, but you won't let on about that. No, you'll come back and you'll say it was lah-de-bloody-dah, saw the Queen and all that nonsense. No one ever tells the truth about overseas travel. Where do you go after Pommyland?'

'Well,' said the Fencer, 'this will surprise you, I guess, but like a lot of bushmen I read avidly, and I mainly read books about art and artists. I've always had this great yearning to see the *Mona Lisa*, so after London I'm off to Paris, to the Louvre, the famous art gallery.'

'Ye Gods! Paris! What a dump! If you want art galleries, mate, there are seven in Alice Springs. Why you'd want to go to Paris, I wouldn't know. You'll have Froggies breathing garlic over you and robbing you blind, and as for their tucker! So where to after Paris?' The Barber was really getting vitriolic.

'I'm a sports lover, too,' replied the Fencer, 'so after Paris I'm going to Spain to see a bullfight. Should be a lot of fun.'

'Bullfight! Bullfight! There's no "fight" mate. It's wholesale bloody slaughter, very unskilfully executed. If you want to see a quick, clean job, whip out to the abattoirs tomorrow morning, and save yourself a lot of money. Definitely give Spain a big miss! They talk a foreign lingo there, and they hate Australians since the Armada. Furthermore, old feller, I happen to know that you're a Catholic and I just bet you're off to Rome on this expensive jaunt, aren't you?'

Yes, the Fencer is just that, a very devout Catholic, and now he was mad. He dodged the flailing scissors, and reached for his travel wallet. He grabbed out his big folder of tickets. 'Yes, I am going to Rome if that's OK,' he roared, brandishing the tickets, 'and if you have a look in here you'll find that Maree Kilgariff has been able to book me an excursion which includes a papal audience. Not an individual audience, of course, but I'll be in a group which sees the Pope at St Peter's!'

Well, the Barber nearly lopped off an ear he was

laughing so much. 'A papal audience!' he shouted. 'You'll be in St Peter's Square with a hundred thousand other stupid tikes, the Pope will give you a bit of a wave, and you'll bore us shitless for the rest of your life telling us you've had a papal audience. Forget the whole flaming nonsense.' The haircut was finished. 'And that'll be $9.50 for the haircut.'

The Fencer paid up and stalked out. 'I don't care what you say,' he called from the door. 'I'm taking this trip, and I reckon it'll be a beauty.' And away he went.

Ten weeks later he arrived back in Alice Springs. He checked at Dalgety's and there was a big fencing contract lined up for him at Argadargada, a big run on the Queensland side. It meant he'd be out bush for about eight weeks, so he thought, 'I'd better have a haircut if I'm going to be away from town that long.'

Down to the Barber he went, and the Barber was at the door holding his comb and scissors, a big smirk on his dial. 'Come in, come in,' said the Barber unctuously, 'and tell me, tell me, tell me, how was the big overseas jaunt old chap?'

The old Fencer settled into the chair. 'Well,' he began slowly, 'as a matter of fact it was tremendous. Let me give you the detail of what happened. First, I went to London. The weather was perfect, the English people were friendliness itself. And yes, not to disappoint you, I did see the Queen. It happened like this. There I was in Pall Mall, right by the Victoria Monument, and down the Mall they came, the Coldstream Guards, the Grenadier Guards, and there's cymbals clashing and brass bands blaring, and thousands of people waving their Union Jacks, me included. And then, riding a beautiful big bay horse, riding side-saddle, came Her Majesty the Queen, and as she rode

25

past she waved, at me. So, I just sort of waved back, and, I'll tell you what. Pomp and circumstance will do me, any time.

'But, if that wasn't enough, then I went to Paris, and . . . oooh-la-la! It was haute couture, and haute cuisine and lots of other hautes as well. And there I was, a battler like me, an old fencer, and I'm in the Louvre, within spitting distance of the *Mona Lisa*. I was transfixed. Couldn't move for a half hour. I just stood there, looking at that smile, and wondering what da Vinci had in mind as he painted that enigmatic face. Eventually I tore myself away, and in the next gallery . . . *Venus de Milo*! Later, I sat in one of those sidewalk restaurants, and there was an accordion player. And as I sat there smoking a Gaulois and sipping my third Pernod, I marvelled at the fact that here I was, in the cultural capital of the world. It was overwhelming.

'But next I went to Spain. Ah, España. Olé! What an experience! There I was, in the bullfighting stadium, a wonderful seat in the front row, a perfect view of everything. There was an awesome sense of excitement, and exotic food smells wafted over the vast arena. Suddenly a fanfare of trumpets, and down through a tunnel into the arena came this noble black bull, pawing the ground. Another fanfare, and into the arena they came, ever so proudly, the toreador, and the picador, and . . . the matador! Then, it's surge, thrust, darts, swirling capes, roars from the crowd. What a spectacle!'

Well, you could hear a pin drop in the Barber's shop. Everyone was spellbound.

The Fencer continued. 'But,' . . . he chose his words carefully, and addressed himself direct to the Barber, 'you were definitely right about Rome. Yes. On the day of the

... er ... papal audience there were, pretty much as you predicted, a hundred and twenty thousand people in St Peter's Square, and it was stinking hot. There were chairs, but I finished up in the third back row, and fifteen places in from the centre aisle. After an interminable wait – and there was no food, no drink – away in the distance, on a balcony, emerged this tiny little figure clad in white. It was His Holiness the Pope all right, but from where I was sitting he looked about the size of a postage stamp. Anyway, he briefly addressed us in Latin, which I don't understand, he blessed us, and then he turned as though to go back into the papal palace. Well, I thought to myself, the Barber got this one right. A bit of a disappointment, to say the least. But then His Holiness stopped, and turned to face us again. Suddenly he walked down from the balcony, down to the square itself, and slowly, every so slowly, he began to walk along the red-carpeted centre aisle, blessing each individual row of people as he passed through the vast crowd. Eventually he came to my row, the third last row, and he stopped. His Holiness stopped! "Excuse me," he said to the first lady in our row, and he blessed her – just her, mind – and then began to walk . . . *along my row* . . . blessing each person individually. And I'm watching out of the corner of my eye. As he came near me I knelt, ready for the blessing. It's my turn! He stood in front of me, His Holiness the Pope, his arms extended in a papal blessing. And as I looked up to him, he looked right into my eyes and said, "What a bloody shocking haircut!"'

The
Two-bottle
Bog

H E WAS FOUR FOOT TEN in his high-heeled riding
boots and weighed eight stone wringing wet. His
name was Jimmy Gibbs and he lived a hundred and
fifty something miles out of town on the border of the big
Aboriginal reserve. He'd come into the country as a tin
gouger and he'd worked on the Westaway field. Struck a
few reasonable pockets and finished up with a cattle
station. Well, it eventually became a cattle station but old
Jim was looking the goanna in the eye for a few years I can
tell you. That's why he always had a good word for a

battler and would slip a quid into the fist of the most unlikely-looking death adder at times: reckoned a man should never forget what it was like to have the arse out of his tweeds.

Didn't drink all that much out on the station, Jimmy, but he gave the grog a real hammering any time he walked a mob into Jindoorie, or came to town for stores or the annual races or the Show. The townies all knew him and they used to get a great kick out of having old Jim perched up on a stool at Bartholomew's Boozer, telling outrageous lies and singing some of his dreadful songs. His feet wouldn't even touch the floor, but that didn't affect his prowess as a drinker: he'd prop there for days on end. If he happened to drop off to sleep on the stool nobody worried. He'd wake up in half an hour or so and you could predict that he'd immediately want to know whose turn it was to shout.

A new demon came to town one Show time, and naturally he didn't know old Jim. When he saw this little joker asleep at the bar the copper reckoned he was full, so he marched Jim out and heaved him up on the back of the police truck. No sooner had the copper gone off to lumber some more drunks that Jim came weaving back inside. Four separate times the copper wheeled him out and back the little fellow would come, with a little bit more hide knocked off each time. Albert Cannon bobbed into the pub for his first beer of the day, not knowing what had happened to Jim.

'How yer enjoyin' the Show, old feller?' said the innocent Albert.

'Not too bad, Albert,' replied Jim, 'but I keep fallin' down a bloody great hole every time I go for a leak!'

Finally duty would call and Jim would load up his old

truck at Fitzgerald's. On they'd go, the wet season supplies: hundred and fifties of flour, seventies of sugar,
forty-fours of petrol, chests of tea, a bag of salt, cases of
jam and treacle, plug tobacco, dried fruit, boiled lollies
and cordial for 'blackfellow Christmas', dresses, trousers
and shirts, calico, saddle blankets, tyres, a pump-jack, and
half a dozen Aboriginals discharged from hospital. And
don't forget five cases of rum for his nibs, Jim Gibbs.

A last round of drinks and away on his hazardous trip.
Drive that way today and you'd think this story was a pack
of lies, but in Jim's day there were about twenty places
where you'd bog a duck after half an inch of rain. With
the old fellow's propensity for staying in town too long
he sometimes got caught by the early storm – look out
then for the Tandangal black-soil flats. Tandangal! 'Damn
Tangle' we called it.

You have to be philosophical about things like bogs in
the bush. There's no point in kicking the truck or biting
your arm, or if-ing and but-ing: you're there and you're
down to the axles, and that's it. Jim was usually fairly
serene about things, but he was meticulous about record-
ing the details of the various 'situations' he'd copped, so he
evolved a formula to enable him to describe matters
succinctly to people who asked what sort of a trip he'd had.
His formula was to keep count of the number of bottles of
OP rum he would consume before he'd get the truck
mobile. As his drinking rate was fairly consistent – the only
time you wouldn't call him a steady drinker was when he
was having his first heart-starter in the morning – if Jim
was to tell you he'd been in a four-bottler or a six-bottler,
you'd have a clear idea of how big a grave he'd have dug in
freeing the old truck.

His record was a twenty-seven-bottler, when he went

down at Damn Tangle after staying in town too long. There'd been a freak early storm of six inches. To make matters worse, Jim had left his shovel behind after a fairly unspectacular three-bottler back at the Jump-up and he had to dig the truck out with a frying-pan. So it's not in the *Guinness Book of Records*, or anything like that, but it's a reasonable feat nonetheless.

We were sitting under a big ironwood tree one day and Jim was telling us about one particular bog which had been difficult to resolve. 'It was funny last wet season,' he said, and we listened expectantly. 'I'd been in town on the sherbet, and I'd stayed too long as usual. Well, going out home I've been bogged quite a few times and me rum supplies are down to two bottles of the old OP. I comes to the Flying Fox and not unexpectedly she's run a banker the previous night. I took a good fast run at her, but I still got bogged comin' up that steep bank on the other side. You know that gluey bit?'

'Yairs,' we said. Jim lit his pipe, tapped his pannikin and waited. Charlie took the hint and splashed a bit of rum into it.

Jim continued. 'Yes, well there I am stuck with only the two bottles left and quite a few trouble spots before I get home. I gets out of the truck to assess the situation and I says to meself: "Gibbs, old chap, is this a one-bottle bog or a two-bottle bog?" Keeping in mind, of course, the very relevant fact that I've only got two bottles left, I thinks I'll be a bit cunning and make her a one-bottler so that if I get stuck again along the track I'll still have a drink left. Right, the decision is made: a one-bottler she is. First I got out me pannikin. Then I knocked the scab off the bottle of rum and I got into it. Down she goes. Real fast. A bit too fast, and perhaps the old brain cells got a bit scrambled in the process. Having consumed the fiery spirit I then grabbed me shovel and dug the mud away from the back wheels. Next I jacked up the truck, cut a few bushes and logs, and corduroyed the road. She looked pretty good. I hopped in behind the steering-wheel, switched on the ignition, pressed the starter, and the engine surged into life. I slapped her into gear. Low, low, slow, slow, I reminded meself, and gave her the herbs. But brr-rr-rr-rr-rr-rr slurp! she went, and ground straight down into that mud again, bogged on every bloody wheel.'

'Gawd,' said Charlie.

'Yes,' said Jim. 'Bogged on every bloody wheel. So, very slowly, and with great composure, I got out of that truck, and I walked to the driver's side front mudguard where there was a rear-vision mirror. I looked into that mirror, and do you know what I said?'

'No,' I croaked. My voice had gone.

Jim paused, then went on, 'I looked into that mirror, looked myself straight in the eye, and I said: "Gibbs, you bloody idiot. You should have known that was a two-bottle bog!"'

A Skinner for the Books

IF YOU'VE BEEN to Normanton or Onslow or Euabalong or Marree you'll know the sort of town I'm talking about. If you haven't ... Well, for starters there's a wide dirt road through the middle of the town. There are some dried-up women, some sweaty, red-faced men, and dozens of agile bare-footed kids who dart around in the dust like a mob of goannas. There's the general store, where they still sell boiled lollies in newspaper cones. There's the baker's shop where they bake those 'high tin' loaves that you cut into thick slices and plaster with butter and apricot jam, as your mouth drools and your nostrils pull in great sniffs of hot, crusty delight. There's the shire hall, established 1913. The pub. The police station. And there are a couple of dozen weatherboard homes with peeling brown paint, and oleanders in every front yard. The donkeys and goats have eaten everything else that ever looked like garden material. Oh, except for a few drought-stricken cedar trees planted by Alderman Ransford back in – when was it? But they're no good for shade or anything, except to serve as perches for the crows and targets for the local mongrels as they cock their legs for one another.

The town has its moments, of course. Remember the night old Christie won a thousand on the Stradbroke? The time that young Tommy Quinn let the black snake go in the women's dunny? And when that big mob of socialites came up for Judy Morrison's wedding at Myall Downs? Most of the time it's pretty quiet, though. But we like it – better than the cities, we reckon.

Malone was one of those blokes. You know the type. He'd been in the army and he'd knocked around the scrub ever since. He had those capable bushman's hands which said he could have a go at just about anything; and he had that funny sort of twinkle in his eyes which made him as alert as a fox terrier. And about as stirry too, if you ever got him going. Used to make a bit of a job of himself on the booze and he probably had a wife and kids back in Perth or Melbourne, but not a bad bloke really. The bush is full of them.

He was always on the lookout for a lurk, so when he came to town he instinctively headed for the pub. To his amazement and delight he discovered there was no SP bookie in town, so he squared it with the publican and the local cop and organised himself to go into business on the following Saturday. The usual deal: ten per cent to the Flying Doctor Service, and a quid each way for the copper on the favourite in the last race.

You have to spend a quid to make a quid, so Malone ordered ten plates of assorted sandwiches – Vegemite or corned beef – from Mrs Halloran opposite the shire hall, borrowed Charlie Dixon's portable radio, and got one of the kids to pinch some white cardboard from the school and cut it into betting tickets. The kid did a great job of stamping with a cut-out potato, producing a very impressive T. MALONƎ. REƆ. BOOʞ. on each one, so he offered the kid an extra point on any nag he wanted to back during the first day's betting.

But to Malone's dismay the races were cancelled owing to the floods in the city. Floods, mind you, when here he was in this dry dusty hole with ten plates of fly-blown sandwiches, a bunch of ringers from Mulga Downs and most of the townspeople with their pockets full of money and no bloody races. He'd have to think quickly.

Suddenly it hit him. Hats. He'd run a book on hats. More specifically, he'd take bets about the type of hat worn by the first person to enter the bar after three o'clock. So he bought a schooner of beer, helped himself to two of his quickly drying sandwiches, and began to ponder the odds.

Ringers' hats, ten-gallon variety, would of course be odds-on favourites. OK, six to four on for ringers' hats. Straw hats? Lots of cockies and road workers around, so a strong possibility: right, straws two to one against. Felt Akubras, fairly popular with all the old RSL fellows, fours. Panamas – might get the odd tourist, let's see, ten to one the Panamas. Pommy-type caps, hardly likely but then you

never could tell with Pommies, fifteens. Oh, there were a couple of Afghans living down on the creek. Turbans, fifty to one. They'd never come near the pub, no risk, but some mug punter might squander a few bob.

Prices on the board, gents, prices on the board. Yes, *faites vos jeux, messieurs.* (He'd learnt that one in the army.) Come on lads, get into them lovely sangers and have a wager with Terry Malone, the punter's friend. What's that, Les? Will I give you an extra point on straws? For you mate, yes, you've got five on to win fifteen on the straw titfers and good luck to you. Who's next? Yes, mate? Hats of your selection but not on the board? Twenties upwards. What's your fancy? Bowlers! You've got fifty pound to your one on the bowler hat, with or without *Times* and brolly, old cobber. And the next please, gents. Prices on the board.

It's going off better than expected, Malone thought as the time drew near three o'clock. Taken a hundred and sixty quid altogether. Let's see, he was holding a fair bit of money on straws so he'd better let ringers' hats out to evens. Even money on the ringers' hats. An even tenner, Clive? Set. Like it again? On.

Five minutes to three. Place your bets please, gents. Final bets. There was a bit of a flurry from one corner of the bar, but this was just a group of two-bob tourists betting on felts. They thought the whole affair was a nice little touch of Australiana, they said. Gawd, they bung it on, those tourists. But the publican didn't mind having the bar jammed full on a Saturday afternoon, so all in all it was going well.

'Right now, gents, I'm declaring the book closed at this point, seeing as how it is three o'clock. The wagers will be finalised when the next person wearing a hat enters this bar. The publican will be the judge in case of disputes, and no correspondence will be entered into. Now, I must ask that nobody leave the bar.'

Here's hoping, thought Malone. Tom Fisher wished he'd gone to the toilet before three o'clock. Wally Fogarty surprised everybody by shouting out of turn. Talk about nerves. After a full minute had gone by, with nobody coming through the door, the palms began to get sweaty, the conversations were more subdued and every eye was glued on that doorknob.

Two minutes. Three. A crow carked out on the road, but otherwise not a sound. Five minutes, and the suspense was starting to tell on a few of them. Malone's hand trembled as he lit a new cigarette from his previous one. He took a deep puff and tried to look nonchalant. Nonchalant! He'd felt more relaxed in a New Guinea foxhole.

Footsteps! Coming to the pub! No mistake. The owner of the feet was ten yards away from the door of the public bar and walking briskly, so there was no doubt about it. This person was heading for the boozer. Would the owner of the feet be the owner of a hat?

Five yards. Three. Up the two wooden steps. A pause. Checking the funds probably, or looking to see that his fly was done up. Yes, the door handle was . . . turning. Come in you lovely wearer of a hat, they all hoped. Come in and win me my bet, please, please.

There was a hat. And what a hat. In the incredible hush Malone jumped up on the bar.

'I'll shout for the mob,' he roared. 'A skinner for the books. A skinner for the books. You bloody beeyeauty!'

The little figure in grey merged with the stunned drinkers.

'*War Cry*, sir? Get your *War Cry*.' Strange. No takers today. Usually sold quite a few in the hotel back home on a Saturday afternoon. They seemed funny people, the drinkers up this way, she thought to herself. And weren't they quiet?

'*War Cry*, sir? Get your *War Cry*.'

The
Man from
Humpty Doo

IN THE LATE FIFTIES, at the delightfully named place
Humpty Doo, just south of Darwin, an attempt was
made to grow rice on a large scale on the Adelaide
River plains. A company called Territory Rice was established and huge investment was forthcoming, particularly
from the United States. The rice grown was superb, but
there was one insuperable problem; the magpie geese
thought all their Christmases had come at once. They ate
the rice as fast as it grew, and nothing could beat them.
Everything was tried – alarms, guns fired at regular

intervals, teams of hunters – but alas! It was one of the many boom-and-bust agricultural ventures undertaken in the Northern Territory over the last century. Understandably all sorts of jokes and tall stories were circulated, and I wrote this piece about a particular bloke who shall remain nameless. But you know the type: you've all met him.

I've rolled me swag in lots of camps,
From Queensland to the West,
I've met with lots of outback champs,
But the oldest and the best
Was a bloke I met at Skewesy's Pub,
We drank a rum or two,
He was mustering geese away up north,
At a place called Humpty Doo.

And he said: 'I've been around a bit,
And I'll show you a trick or two,
Take a gander at me gaggle of geese,'
Said the man from Humpty Doo.

I watched him breakin' in a goose,
But he couldn't ride for nuts
He was useless as a rouseabout,
And as a cook he'd rot yer guts.
But he said he'd rode with Skuthorpe,
Shorn sheep with Jackie Howe,
He'd been a chef at Menzies,
And he'd milked the sacred cow.

Crutchin' geese was not his line,
Couldn't stand the dags,
But he was a champ at bludgin' drinks

42

And smokin' OP fags.
And he said he'd dug the Murray,
Won a VC at Tobruk,
Said he'd fought Les Darcy,
And sailed with Captain Cook.

He built a yard to brand his geese,
And he made me laugh like hell,
'Cos he tried to make some post-holes,
By chopping up a well.
But he said that he'd rode Phar Lap,
Played for Collingwood in the ruck,
Played Davis Cup with Laver,
And bowled Bradman for a duck.

He said he'd groomed Gough Whitlam,
Been a TV star,
Travelled with Slim Dusty,
And owned a pub at Marble Bar.
But if you tallied up these things,
Mate, I'm 'tallying' you
He was just two hundred years of age,
The man from Humpty Doo.

But like he said, 'I've been around a bit,
And I'll show you a trick or two,
Just take a gander at me gaggle of geese,'
Said the man from Humpty Doo.

The Borroloola Hermits

THEY WERE straight out of a Steinbeck novel. I had
been at Borroloola, in the Gulf region, only a couple
of days when a joker said to me, 'Are you going to
the church service on Sunday?'

Now I'd been around a bit so I knew he wasn't talking
about your actual church service, but a drink. 'Bloody
oath,' I responded. 'Where's she on?' He told me to be at
Albert Morcom's camp, under the mango trees, at about
9.30 a.m.

I duly arrived, and there they were, sitting in a big ring,

most of them propped on army cyclone beds taking it easy. The Borroloola Hermits. They motioned me to sit down, which I did, not knowing quite what to expect. Suddenly someone passed me a bottle of metho, indicating that it was my turn to have a swig. Gawd, I thought, this is a nice bunch of deros, so I declined the offer and passed the bottle to the bloke next to me. He took an almighty pull at the bottle, and introduced himself as Fred Morris, better known as 'the Whispering Baritone'. I subsequently established that some of them had very fancy nicknames, most of these beautifully appropriate to their personalities. There was 'the Reluctant Saddler', 'the Freshwater Admiral', 'the Mad Fiddler', and 'the White Stallion' – he was a lecherous old missionary who had had a dishful of flour emptied over him when a female missionary discovered him seducing one of the Aboriginal girls at the mission.

But back to the metho. I thought at the outset that I would leave them to their dereliction, but suddenly they launched into a most erudite debate. I forget the topic on that given day, but rest assured I went on subsequent Sundays to enjoy the proceedings. They were quite well informed and articulate, all being graduates of the Borroloola Library. I had arrived fifty years after a police constable had written to the Carnegie Institute in the United States, bemoaning the fact that he had been posted to this dreadful place called Borroloola. To the constable's delight the Yanks responded by sending chests full of leather-bound classic books. In his wisdom the policeman decided that the best place for the Borroloola Library was the gaol. So one's best chance of getting a good education lay in the prospect of the odd stretch in the slammer. And you name it, they'd done it – poddy dodging, supplying liquor to Aboriginals, the odd bit of general skulduggery.

45

Along the way they'd read the books, pinched some of them and shared them around the Loo – which is what Borroloola is affectionately called. So the local level of scholarship was extremely high, with Albert Morcom, Andy Anderson and Roger Jose being the star performers.

Ah, Roger Jose. The daddy of them all. I can see him now. He used to delight in delivering great bursts of Virgil's *Aeneid* in Latin, or of *The Rubaiyat of Omar Khyyam*, and one wonderful day he held us spellbound as he compared, in the most eloquent English I have ever heard, the relative merits of Gray and Browning. To my dismay I heard a couple of local jokers – definitely not numbered among the Borroloola Hermits – refer to Roger as 'the Death Adder', and I thought to myself, 'How dare you: the Death Adder, with all those connotations of poison and treachery.' How dare they! Away, dreadful sobriquet.

On the basis of his great scholarship Roger had developed fascinating, if somewhat eccentric, theories. He had a theory, for example, about housing. He said one day, 'We live in a cyclonic region here at the Loo, so everybody should live in round homes. Then, if a cyclone blows your house over, you can roll along in it.' To prove his point Roger built a beautiful split-level home from two old rainwater tanks. The ground floor of his home was a 10 000 gallon tank, upturned. Wired to the top was a 5000 gallon tank, which served as the mezzanine. Out the back he had a 1000 gallon job which was the dunny, but Roger wouldn't use crude words like dunny so he called the outhouse 'the amenities block'. A great man for euphemisms.

He also had a theory about clothing. He reckoned that if you wanted to keep a waterpipe cool you covered it, so in the middle of the wet season at the Loo, when it was stinking hot, he would wear two or three of those old short-sleeved flannel singlets your grand-dad wore, with an army greatcoat over the top. And he used to pull over his head one of those striped pillow-cases, with holes cut for his eyes and mouth. Yes, he did look a bit odd, but he reckoned he kept cool. Every morning he'd go to the spring to get two buckets of water. He'd carry them on the old Chinamen's yoke, the bamboo pole, and he looked magnificent.

But Roger's most interesting theory related to the poison strychnine. He had read in the classics that the ancient Egyptians and Aztecs had developed the capacity to take various poisons in small doses as a heart stimulant. When I was first told about Roger taking strychnine for the same purpose I didn't believe it, but I was to see it with my own eyes.

One day Hector Anderson and I rode out and we killed a bullock. We cut it up and I saved a bit of fresh beef, and a bit of salf beef as well, for Roger. I took the meat over to his tank the next morning. As I approached the tank I spotted the old bloke, sitting alone and talking to himself. I waited for him to finish the earnest conversation he was having, and then I walked up and delivered the meat. He thanked me and then said, in his inimitably quaint way, 'One often sits here and craves one of the master's oxen, but far too often one has to content oneself with slaughter-ing another poor unfortunate marsupial.'

I observed that I had spotted him talking to himself. He said, 'Ah, yes, I do a lot of that.' Then he looked shrewdly at me and went on. 'Since I developed my superiority complex, I find it stimulating to talk to an intelligent person for a change.'

That should have shut me up, but with the impetuosity of youth I determined to satisfy my curiosity about the strychnine. I said, as nonchalantly as possible, 'The locals tell me you take the occasional dose of strychnine, Roger?'

'Oh, yes,' he responded, 'I take it regularly, for the old ticker. Have done for years.'

It was a bit rude of me I know, intruding thus on the old bloke's privacy, but I asked him if I could watch the next time around. He told me to come over the following Tuesday. So at 9 a.m., by appointment, I fronted. To my surprise he took me to the middle of the nearby Borroloola airstrip. Why out here?

'You wouldn't want to risk bumping your head on a tree when you take the stuff, son,' was his reply.

Then he swallowed a teaspoonful of strychnine, jumped and shivered a bit, and indicated that I should check his heartbeat. Boom, boom, boom.

What a man. I wrote my first-ever song about Roger. Here's a bit of it:

In another place, another age,
Roger would have been treated as a sage,
Plato and Socrates, out at the Loo
Would probably be called 'death adders' too.
Roger liked astrology, history, anthropology,
Poetry, politics and theology,
Geography, philosophy, he fancied all of these,
And he liked to sit and argue underneath the shady trees.

He'd a long grey beard and a glittering eye,
But Roger never, ever, worked for a boss,
A long grey beard and a glittering eye,

49

But he wouldn't have shot the albatross.
For Roger liked to drink a little metho with his dinner
A spoonful of strychnine was certainly a winner,
A rum and a johnny-cake served for his tea,
And he said: 'Borroloola is the place for me.'

The
Meanest Man
I Ever Met

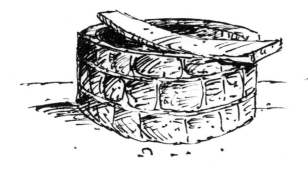

P EOPLE TALK ABOUT the hospitality of the outback, the generosity of bush people, and by and large it's a fact: you have to learn to share in small communities, because one day it might be you with the arse out of your tweeds. But occasionally you get a mean person, and I'd like to tell you about the meanest man I ever met.

Tom Burrows and I had taken a contract to do a bit of yard-building – you know, the old post-and-rail stuff – on this bloke's property. I won't tell you his full name, but his first name was Bill. He had sent word to us to be on the property on the Sunday evening, ready for what he called an early start on the Monday morning. Well, we got there at about half-past four on the Sunday arvo, and I asked him if he would show us the men's quarters. Down we went and you should have seen the place. A rusty old shed, full of cobwebs and spiders, no electricity, a cold shower, two cyclone beds (no mattresses, pillows, sheets, blankets) and a long-drop dunny 200 yards down the flat.

'What time's the evening meal?' I had the temerity to ask.

'You're not my responsibility until tomorrow,' he grunted, and Burrows and I looked gloomily at one another. We decided that sleep might take away our hunger pains, so we lay on these two cyclone-wire beds like a couple of stiffs, and that's what we quickly were, because it was *freezing*!

At 3 a.m. precisely, on the Monday morning, in stormed old Bill. 'Get out of bed you lazy so-and-sos!' he roared, 'here it is three o'clock Monday morning, the day after tomorrow's Wednesday, half the bloody week gone and nothing down. Get up!'

We bounded to our feet. 'What about breakfast?' I was stupid enough to ask. 'Have a good drink of that beautiful fresh water as you clean your teeth, son,' he said to me, 'but do it quickly, there's yard-building to be done – or had your forgotten the reason for your holiday?'

He took us down to the yard site, in the darkness, and then he gave us a lecture. 'Now there's one thing I can't stand, and that's bludgers. I expect you to have six panels of this yard finished by lunchtime, and you are not to knock off until twelve o'clock. On the dot, not a second earlier. Then you have an hour for lunch, and I've got a special treat for your lunch – bread and more of that beautiful fresh water, which we get from our well at great expense. So right, get stuck into it, keep those heads down and those arses up. Understand? Six panels by lunchtime, or else!'

Tom and I exchanged hopeless glances. I suppose most of my readers will have done a bit of yard-building over the years, so you'll know that the task he had set us would have been impossible even with power tools, and we had none. We had a crosscut saw, an adze and a brace and bit, and we had to erect the posts, mortice them and fit five adzed rails and then Cobb & Co. wire twitches to hold it all together. You know the sort of thing. Impossible. But we had to try. And do you know what made it worse? Old Bill then went and sat in the shade of a tree, and went to sleep until half past ten. Then he staggered off, heading for the homestead, leaving Tom and I trying to meet his deadline.

His wife saw him coming, and called to him, 'Bill, darling. Bill.'

'What do you want?' he grunted. He was not only mean, he was an ill-mannered old bugger to boot.

'Oh Bill, I'm glad you've come. I was just out at the well, trying to pump some water to make you a cup of tea, but I'm afraid the pump's broken. Could you fix it please, dear?'

'Oh, alright,' he said with bad grace, and over he went to the well. Now this well was 150 feet deep down to the water, but Bill was so mean he wouldn't have a windmill or a pump-jack to pump the water. Oh, no. He had a platform erected over the top and across the well, just a single plank, and his poor wife had to climb out onto this plank and hand-pump, would you believe, hand-pump the water up from a depth on 150 feet. And he charged her three bob a kettle-full! I told you he was mean, didn't I?

Well, he spotted that a bolt had broken on the pump, so he got a new bolt and he had to clamber out onto the platform to insert it. He had a shifting spanner in one hand and the bolt in the other, and he was carefully walking out on the plank when, you guessed it, he lost his balance.

'Yaa-aa-aagh,' he yelled, as he disappeared and went hurtling down into the darkness where, 150 feet down, he finished with an almighty splash in the freezing water. It was really deep, and he was a poor swimmer. Well, he paddled, trod water furiously, and shouted, 'Help! Help!'

Meanwhile his wife had gone inside the house, where she was ironing some clothes. She heard the faint call for help, and ran outside. Slowly, she identified that the voice was coming from the direction of the well. She ran, flat out, knelt at the outside of the well, and called into the darkness, 'Is there anybody down there?'

'Yes, it's me, you stupid bloody woman,' roared Bill, and his voice had an amazing echo to it. 'Get me out of here!'

Mrs Bill thought, 'What in the hell can I do? I must think of something.' Suddenly, an idea came.

'Bill, dear? Can you hear me?'

'Of course I can bloody well hear you. Get me out of here!'

'Bill, I think I've got a good idea. Shall I run down to the yards, and get those two men to come and give a hand?'

To her surprise old Bill roared back, 'What time is it?' She quickly looked at her watch.

'It's twenty minutes to twelve, darling. Why do you ask?'

'Well,' said Bill, 'I'll swim round for twenty minutes, and they can pull me out in their lunch hour!'

Puftaloons, Macaroons and Other High Risers

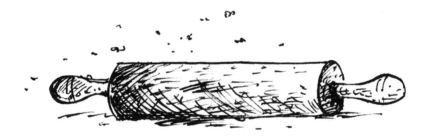

I GUESS YOU'VE HEARD OF GREASY BIGGINS, STATION COOK?
You haven't? Then you'd better take a good look,
On the great big stations where the cattle run,
I think you'll find that nearly everyone
Knows Greasy Biggins, station cook.

He can bake a puftaloon, a dumpling or a macaroon,
A roly-poly puddin' or a bun,
A carpet snake, or a johnny-cake,
Greasy knows a dish for everyone.

It was Greasy who invented 'Biggins buns'
And I think the Anzacs fired them through their guns,
They're the buns that every bushy craves
They're used as doorstops or as tombstones over graves,
Greasy Biggins' famous buns.

Greasy once worked on the Birdsville Track,
Where the ringers all gave cheek and they answered back
So he fixed them when they complained about his faults,
He served them damper made from flour and Epsom Salts,
Greasy Biggins, station cook.

I can still see Greasy Biggins with his pot,
Poised above a stew called 'Cop this Lot'.
The greasy drops of sweat kept rolling in,
'Added flavour,' he told me with a greasy grin,
Greasy Biggins, famous cook.

But despite old Greasy's superb culinary feats,
The ringers once went crook because there were no
    sweets.
So he made a giant strawberry blancmange in an old horse-
    trough,
Stood above 'em with a bloody great axe 'til they knocked
    it all off,
Greasy Biggins, station cook.

Yes, he can bake a puftaloon, a dumpling or a macaroon,
A roly-poly puddin' or a bun,
A carpet snake or a johnny-cake,
Greasy knows a dish for everyone.

I FEEL A BIT GUILTY about writing the above lines about the late John Biggins, for yes, he died recently, and he will be missed in the bush. Sadly missed. He worked on most of the big stations in central Australia, and he was certainly famous. Or perhaps infamous is a better word to describe him.

You see, he was a terribly dirty cook, filthy in fact. And so he acquired his nickname, Greasy Biggins. I can't testify that this is true, but the ringers on one station vowed that he was so greasy, dogs used to lick his shadow.

One true story about G.B. relates to his term of employment at Durrie Station, just east of Birdsville. He was working for the old S.K., the legendary cattle king Sidney Kidman (later Sir Sid). It seems that rumours were floating around the outback about this filthy cook, and Kidman was naturally upset. S.K. decided to go to Durrie and check things out for himself. If Biggins was as repulsive as rumoured, he would have his papers branded NTR – Never To Return – a variation on the old DCM – Don't Come Monday. So Sir Sidney drove in his little truck all the way from Adelaide to Birdsville, then on to Durrie, and all along the way people were talking about only one thing – the filthy cook at Durrie.

By the time Kidman arrived at Durrie he was hopping mad. But he quietly composed himself, parked his truck under the peppercorn trees by the windmill, and sneaked over to the homestead. On tiptoes, he peeped into the kitchen, through the window. There was Greasy Biggins, in the process of making an apple pie. But this was no ordinary apple pie. No, it was a monumental apple pie, for the big muster was on and thirty ringers were attending from the surrounding stations, and Greasy was required to feed them as well as the eight ringers working for

Durrie itself. So he had a savage look on his kisser, and Sidney Kidman was watching his every move through the window.

Biggins rolled out a layer of pastry the size of a double blanket, giving his nose a bit of a wipe with the back of his hand in the process. Splat! He hurled the pastry into the great big pie dish. Ten shovelfuls of dried apples were then flung on top, followed by an entire 70 lb bag of sugar. Kidman was watching every move, taking in every detail. Biggins rolled out another layer of pastry, garnished with a 'bushman's fling', and slapped that on the top of the apple and sugar. The pie was almost ready for the oven. But first, a couple of epicurean embellishments. Greasy grabbed a carving knife, wiped it carefully on the seat of his dungarees, and neatly trimmed the pastry.

That was enough for Sidney Kidman. He headed for the door, about to administer the chop. But the cattle king of Australia was in for another shock. As he stormed into the kitchen Biggins was into the final stage. You've seen your mother do it as she bakes an apple pie: the final step is to take a fork, punch a few random holes in the top of the pie. Then, using the fork, you crimp the pastry against the edge of the pie dish. You've seen Mum do that, haven't you? It helps to seal the flavour in, and the pie comes out of the oven with a nice crinkly look to it. Just as Sidney Kidman burst into the kitchen Greasy was in the process of crimping the pastry. But he wasn't using a fork, was he? No! As the cattle king of Australia watched in shocked silence Biggins took out his false teeth, top and bottom sets, and attacked the pie. Clack, clack clack, clack, clack the teeth chattered as they were directed around the edge of the pie by a now more-contented G.B., another master-piece about to be launched. Clack, clack, clack, and very artistically, too.

59

Kidman was furious, and finally recovered the power of speech. 'You filthy brute,' he roared, 'You rotten bounder. How dare you! I've heard all about you, Biggins, and it's all absolutely true, obviously. You swine. Haven't you got a tool you could use to do that job?'

Greasy was nonplussed. His reply was tinged with a level of sadness at having his life's labour put under scrutiny. Haughtily he responded, 'Yes, of course I have, Mr Kidman, but I'm saving that for the doughnuts.'

The Old S.K.

TALKING ABOUT Greasy Biggins and his run-in with Sidney Kidman reminds me of a few things that are bandied around the bush about the cattle king himself. Everybody knows that the fifteen-year-old Kidman left Kapunda in South Australia with ten bob and a one-eyed horse named Cyclops. He became incredibly rich and powerful, mainly as a buyer and seller of properties. He'd buy when prices were rock-bottom, and he'd sell when they were sky-high. He rarely improved stations, but was a fairly ruthless exploiter. And he was a very astute businessman.

Kidman surrounded himself with some of the greatest bushmen this country will ever know. They came to be called 'the Kidman Men', with capital letters. Principal among these were Pratt, his buyer, and Arch McLean and 'Charlie the Rager', his principal drovers. Kidman finished up owning cattle stations from the Gulf of Carpentaria to the Great Australian Bight, over 100 000 square miles of country. At one stage he was negotiating to buy the state of Victoria: he was going to use it as a horse paddock!

Kidman was heavily into religion, and he never drank, smoke or swore. But he was as tough as nails, nonetheless. And mean! Talk about 'scorpions in the kick'! It's said that he issued instructions to his station managers that in the stock camp the treacle tin always had to be positioned near the fire so it would not spread too thickly on the damper. And he once fired a man for using a match to light his pipe. 'We can't afford unnecessary luxuries like matches,' he roared. 'And furthermore, if one of my men's hands are so soft he can't pick a coal from the fire to light his pipe, that tells me he hasn't been working hard enough.' Kidman's motto, appropriately enough, was 'Leave your cheque book at home, and keep your branding iron hot'.

They say that S.K. only ever made one error of judgement, and that was when he sold his founding shareholding in BHP. And that only once was he dudded in a transaction. That was on the day that Micky Woods, one of his employees, caught S.K. on the hop and got 'change of a quid' from the cattle king after passing over a folded jam label. The closest he ever got to swearing was to use the adjective 'jolly', which is a Methodist word meaning 'bloody'. He always referred to children as 'jolly little tinkers'. One day, in a fit of generosity, he chartered a little rail-motor to take some children from the Salvation Army Orphanage for a picnic in the Adelaide Hills. The children were put on the little train and then Kidman's truck arrived. On the back were two boxes, and S.K. gave instructions that the boxes should be loaded. 'What's in the boxes?' somebody asked. 'There's bread in this one,' replied Kidman, 'and treacle in this one.' And then he confided, 'Those jolly little tinkers, they just love sweets.'

One other brush between S.K. and a jolly little tinker occurred in the railway trucking yards at Marree in South Australia. They were sending a trainload of bullocks to the Adelaide market – mainly old pikers who hadn't been mustered since they were first branded, and were they wild! They were impossible to handle, and being short-handed Kidman himself hopped into the task of trying to draft the cattle. He was down in the yards when suddenly out of the corner of his eye he saw a big, mad-eyed bullock lining him up. The bullock pawed the ground for a bit, and then, no respecter of the rich and powerful, charged. Kidman took off, the bullock after him. Round and round the yard they went with the bullock getting closer and closer, and the cattle king getting desperate, looking for some form of escape. There was an urchin sitting on the top rail of the yard, a snotty-nosed ten-year-old freckled monster who was enjoying this intensely. 'Run Kidman, run!' roared the kid, and the cattle king did just that. Talk about run! Round and round the yard, and the bullock was almost in goring mode, as they say in the classics. 'Run for your life, Kidman,' advised the delighted urchin, who hadn't had such fun since the day they fed Grandpa the lamington made from sponge rubber. Eventually Kidman decided that the only escape route was upward, so he took an almighty leap for the top rail of the yard. He just made it, and there was the cattle king of Australia dangling over the top rail, out of breath and looking most undignified and dishevelled. The bullock was a couple of feet below him, its nostrils flaring, its red eyes blazing, pawing the ground, unconquered. Kidman eventually regained some composure and looked around him and down at the bullock, still ready to demolish him. Then alongside him he spotted this grinning urchin.

'And as for you, you jolly little tinker,' he roared, 'I'll have you know, you're not allowed to call me Kidman. I have a handle to my name.'

'You bloody near had one up your arse', replied the urchin.

Another time at Marree they were trucking a consignment of Kidman stock to Adelaide. This time it was donkeys. There was a demand for donkey meat for smallgoods somewhere or other, and Kidman had instructed that they muster some of the wild donkeys running on one of his stations. Down came the station master, prepared to have a dig at this strange consignment being sent away by Australia's famous cattle king. By this time it was *Sir* Sidney Kidman, if you don't mind.

'And what are we trucking today, Sir Sidney?' asked the devious station master.

But S.K. was much too smart for him. 'A trainload of station masters,' was the quick reply.

Marsupial Joe

IT WAS 'WAY OUT WEST' IN A MINING TOWN
And old Prospector Joe
Rattled up the road in his battered old truck
From his outback mining show.
He breasted the bar, and he ordered a beer,
And he counted out his dough,
But the publican said, 'You're threepence short,
And I reckon you'll have to go.'

Joe pulled a tobacco tin out of his kick
As he walked towards the door.
He looked at the publican in disgust,
Said, 'Mate, you think I'm poor,
But in this tin are "samples", mate,
And I am fairly sure
I'll have no financial worries, mate,
From now to ever more.'

With the incredible speed of insatiable greed,
The publican was heard to say,
'Joe, old pal, old cobber, old friend,
I'd love to have you stay.
We'll have a few free drinks and meals,
We'll send your samples for "assay"
And we'll form a mining company,
This very blooming day.'

Well, the rumour spread like wildfire,
The locals filled the bar,
They shouted Joe exotic drinks
And he puffed a big cigar,
The sheilas all proposed to him,
Folks came from near and far,
They formed a mining company,
And they called it 'Western Star'.

Joe wouldn't let the locals
See the contents of his tin,
But as he wrapped it carefully,
He wore a crafty grin.
He went down to the post office,
And he dropped his parcel in,
And the publican stuck as close to Joe
As a plaster on his shin.

They wined Joe, they dined Joe,
They drove him all around,
New tyres and a clutch for his old red truck
To make it safe and sound.
For two full weeks old Joe was king
And he never bought a round,
But when the message came from the School of Mines
He was nowhere to be found.

They searched for Joe both high and low,
But he'd flown off like a bird,
So the publican grabbed Joe's telegram
And demanded to be heard.
He ripped it open, swallowed, gasped,
Then he spluttered out these words:
'Your samples are identified,
As top-grade kangaroo turds!'

International Brinkmanship

I HAD MY FIRST TRIP to the United States recently. One
of a group which represented Australia at the annual
Cowboy Poetry Gathering at Elko, Nevada, I had a
truly wonderful time. As a bonus we went to Los Angeles,
San Francisco, Oklahoma (to the Cowboys' Hall of Fame),
and the thing that impressed more than anything was the
friendliness of the people. And they were sincerely inter-
ested in Australia and the Australian way of life.

When I returned home the very first thing I did was
telephone a mate of mine, and tell him off. 'How dare you

tell me such lies!' I admonished. You see, my mate had contacted me when he heard I was going to the US. His final word of advice was – I'll quote him – 'Watch out for those bloody Yanks, Ted. They're dreadful skites.'

Well, that wasn't my experience at all. Not only did Americans not even understand the word 'skite' – they call such people 'show-offs' or 'braggarts' – but the vast majority of American people I met were quiet and unassuming. Except for one particular bloke. Just the one.

This fellow – who probably could be classified as a skite – was the proprietor of a Mexican restaurant in Los Angeles. We were walking down the street and were attracted to the restaurant via the exotic smells wafting onto the footpath. In we went, and there inside was the owner, stirring the pot whence emanated the smells. It was the biggest pot I'd ever seen – not unlike the big pots they cook missionaries in, in cartoons. And this joker is stirring the pot with a No. 8 shovel. I'm not kidding. Would I lie to you?

We sat at our table, and he must have heard my different accent. He called to me, 'Hey, son. Are you an Aussie?'

'Yes, I am actually,' I responded.

'Come over here and have a look at this,' he invited. So over I went. The smells were mouth-watering.

'What do you think? Have you ever seen anything like this Down Under?' he asked.

I replied, 'I'm certainly impressed. What do you call this, er, dish?'

'We call this "Chile",' he replied. 'People in LA just love Mexican food, and I have to cook a pot this size every day. You wouldn't see its equivalent in Australia, I suppose?'

'Tell me more about it,' I said. 'What are the ingredients, so I can make some comparisons?'

'Well,' he began, 'there's 150 lbs of ground mince beef for a start. Prime quality, of course. Then there's three bags of birdseye chillies – that's what I call the "afterburner", the burning ring of fire sort of thing – three sacks of onions, two huge bags of beans, and then gallons, literally gallons, of special sauces and condiments that I add.' He gave the pot a flamboyant stir with the shovel, and then looked searchingly at me. 'I guess things just don't happen on this sort of scale in Aussie?'

I was getting a bit jack of this bloke. 'Well, we do things on a reasonably large scale,' I said. 'Do you mind if I show you something?'

'Son, you show me anything you goddam well like,' he replied, smugly, stirring away with his shovel.

I quickly ducked back to our table, where I had left my briefcase. Inside, yes, there it was: I thought I had kept it. Slowly I took out a copy of the Queensland newspaper I had been reading on the trip across – the *North Queensland Register* – a famous old journal I've subscribed to for years. I nonchalantly walked back to the stirrer, opening the newspaper as I walked. He was watching me. I came to the Cattle Sales section, and showed him the headline.

'This is how we prepare meals in Australia, mate,' I said, with a bit of flair. And the headline read:

FIFTEEN HUNDRED FAT BULLOCKS
HEADING FOR THE CURRY.

The Chinese Connection

I GET A BIT ANGRY when I hear people arguing against Asian migration to Australia, and I want to introduce the complainants to my dear mate Chin Chui Hoong, sometimes referred to as 'the Flying Chinaman' and generally known by his Anglicised name of Ronald Gordon Chin. He's an Australian whose Chinese forebears came here in the gold-rush days, and 'Hoonger' himself was born at Emungalin, on the north bank of the Katherine River. He's as ocker as Paul Hogan, was a wonderful sportsman in our young days in Darwin, and it was via sport that he acquired his nickname the Flying Chinaman. And you should hear him sing 'Donkey Serenade'!

He took up singing after he gave away boxing. During the Second World War he'd gone from Darwin to Adelaide to join the RAAF. He'd had to wait to a bit, so he got a job carting bags of spuds at the Adelaide markets. Somebody said to him, 'You're a fit young fellow. Do you want to have a go at boxing, down at the Stadium?' Hoonger agreed but he thought his Granny, who was looking after him, would not want her grandson mixed up in the boxing game, so he thought he'd fight under the name of Spud Chang. He was getting the father of a hiding from some joker, who eventually nailed him in a clinch. 'You know, Spud,' said the adversary, 'you're the fastest backward runner I've ever met?' That was it. Singing was a better go, and the world's a richer place . . .

I have lots of wonderful friends among Darwin's Chinese community, and many of them are great humorists, with a definite Chinese twist to their humour. Take Eddy Quong, the man we call 'the Yellow Peril'. When the Humpty Doo rice project was a goer, I said to Eddy one day, 'Which do you prefer, Eddy, the Humpty Doo rice or the Riverina?' Quick as a flash he replied, 'Don't ask me about rice, mate. I only ever had one bowl of the stuff, and look what happened to me eyes and me nose!'

When Chinese babies are born they are usually not 'displayed' for about a month. A mate of Eddy's named Norm Balke wasn't aware of this custom, and he was a bit concerned that he hadn't seen Eddy and Greta's new baby. He took Eddy aside. 'Eddy,' said Norm, 'I haven't seen the new baby. There's, er, nothing wrong with it, is there, mate?' Eddy bounced into the bedroom and produced the baby. 'I'll say there's something wrong with it mate. Have a look. It's a bloody Chinaman'.

Then there was the self-styled 'Mad Chinaman', Jamesy Yuen. One day during the wet season in Darwin I was walking down Wood Street, past Jamesy's house. It was bucketing down. 'Come in out of the rain, Ted, and have a beer,' he called. So we sat under the house and had a 'few drink', as he'd call it. I got him talking about pre-war Darwin, and he had a fund of stories about his grandfather, who had worked on the Pine Creek railway in the gold-rush days. Apparently the Chinese labourers had been engaged at fourpence a day. One day the government boss announced that due to a recession the wages were being cut to twopence a day. So the wily Chinese got hacksaws, and cut the blades of their shovels in half.

I was aware that Jamesy had been a labourer on the Darwin wharf at the time of the Japanese bombing, and I asked him to tell me about it. You've got to remember that this story came from a Darwin Chinese ocker in the best Strine imaginable. 'What was it like?' said Jim. 'Christ, there I am, working, well sort of, on the bloody wharf, and over come the bloody Japs. There's a bloody great explosion, and I'm knocked clean off me bloody feet and I finish up in the Darwin harbour. Well, I'm not a flash swimmer, and there's oil burning in the water, and there's smoke and debris everywhere, but I'm swimming for me life, breast-stroking to where I thought the wharf was. I'm taking in mouthfuls of oily water, covered in grease and shit, and getting really bloody desperate. Suddenly I spots a dinghy, being rowed by two jokers I've been working with for the last fifteen years. I started to swim towards them. I got to within six feet of them, and they saw me. "Quick, Tom, there's a Jap. Hit the bastard," one roared, and they got stuck into me with their paddles!'

We used to have a lot of laughs at the Vic Hotel, which during my days in Darwin was run by the Lim family. The barmen were the four Lim boys, Arthur, Richard, Alex and Gerald. Old Sing used to sit guarding the till, and occasionally George Lim, the boys' father, used to check the pub. I was always a terror for singing, and George used to tell the boys in no uncertain terms to 'Shut that bastard up, he's upsetting the drinkers'. Many years later, when the boys had the Rapid Creek Hotel, it was a joke among us that they used to pay me £500 a night to sing at the pub. The same songs!

Darwin was a great place for (generally illegal) gambling and most popular was an intriguing Chinese game called Pai Kew, played with dominoes and dice. It was heady stuff for a young teenager to watch these games and sometimes have ten bob 'behind' the bet of one of the big gamblers, who might have a thousand pounds up front. They were good about it, the big gamblers like Charlie On, Paul Radomi, Mook Sang, or Jacky Burns. The majority of the really big gamblers were either Greek or Chinese, and it was funny the way they would speak to one another in the foullest language imaginable, using Greek or Cantonese epithets that would make you blush if you heard them translated. But within the ranks of the gamblers it was OK.

The Lim boys had a restaurant at the Vic, and a new Greek bloke came to town. He came into the restaurant, and started to try to impress. He ordered a meal – Alex was serving him – and he finished up by saying, 'And I'll have some flied lice'. Alex gave him such a look. 'Pardon?' said Alex.

'I'll have some flied lice. Isn't that what you Chinese call it?'

Alex put the hands on the hips, a sure sign of fireworks. 'Listen, son,' he said, very calmly, 'I'd like to let you know that I was educated at St Peter's College in Adelaide, and I can say "fried rice" as well as anybody, you Gleek plick!'

Alex, of course, finished up as the Lord Mayor of Darwin, and was loved by everybody. He was a book-maker for a while at the Fannie Bay race-course, and he used to delight everybody on St Patrick's Day by arriving at the course decked out in green, his betting board reading 'Alex O'Lim, Registered Bookmaker'. One St Patrick's Day Alex put on green beer at the pub. A regular drinker with no Irish affiliation came in, and when Alex passed him a schooner of the green beer the drinker looked askance.

'What do you think of the green beer?' said Alex, genial Mine Host.

'It's a bit bloody cloudy,' said your man.

'What do you want, bloody thunder and lightning?' demanded Alex.

And I can't let you go without telling you briefly about the White Chinaman, Henry Lee. In genetic terms Henry is Caucasian, but he was adopted by the Lee family as a baby and reared as a Chinese. Indeed many Chinese say he is the most Chinese person in Darwin. The family, to make the little weak baby strong, gave him the strongest name possible in Chinese terms. They called him Lee Kim Hoong: Lee is the family name, Kim means 'gold' and Hoong means 'red', the strongest colour for Chinese people. Affectionately he is known in Darwin as Fang Quee Doy Hoong, which translates colloquially as White Devil Chinaman.

Henry tells a funny story against himself. Because his first language is Cantonese his English is, as he says himself, 'different'. 'People say to me,' he will tell you, 'what you, Henry, Swedish something?. "No," I say, "I'm a Chinaman." "Bullshit," they say to me. So I give him good swearword, Cantonese, Si Yip, anything.'

He was telling me one day about the wartime. He said,

'Funny one day, two military police come my house. They say to me "You know any boy name Henry Lee?". Silly bugger, I'm tellim "That me, I'm the Henry Lee". You know what they say? They say, "We take you Darwin RSL, you gotta join the army. So they take me to the man, and he say "You swear on the Bible for the King" and I say "I can't do that, I'm Confucian". He say to me "Bullshit, you not bloody Confucian, you prisoner". So they put me in a cage, back of the Darwin RSL. All my mate come and laugh at me, and they say "Join the army, Henry, and you get uniform and two weeks leave". So, alright, I swear the Bible, and you know what they do? They make me military policeman! They send me Melbourne training, and I stop Melbourne Cricket Ground. I think, that good, I got my Chinese uncle there Little Bourke Street, I go visit him. So I got my military police uniform, I go Little Bourke Street. I hear "click click", the fan-tan game, and I knock my uncle door. One Chinaman he open the little grille, he say "You go away you white man" so I say to him "Ho nhe fah sung kai'ai-a" which mean in Cantonese "You stupid prawn-headed bastard" and he say "Ah, we know you, you our boy from Darwin", and they take me in.'

The Barter System

PEOPLE USE the term 'recession' lightly these days, but I wonder if folks really know the meaning of the word 'hardship' in this, the lucky country. I'll acknowledge that those who, like my own parents, experienced the depression of the 1930s would understand, but I don't think it's been quite that bad since those demoralising days.

Mind you, there was a time when my workmate Tom Burrows and I were 'looking the goanna in the eye', as the old bushies say about times when you haven't got the

money to buy tucker, let along grog or tobacco. We'd reverted to the old Australian practice of 'humping the drum' – 'Waltzing Matilda', 'carrying the swag', whatever you like to call it – walking from station to station in the hope that the various owners might take pity on us and give us a bit of work. Anything to earn an honest shilling. Neither of us could contemplate the demeaning experience of going on the 'rock and roll'.

We came to this particular station one day, and the owner was a nice old bloke for whom we'd done a bit of work previously. He could see we were down on our luck, so he suggested that we might extend his little Flying Doctor airstrip by a couple of hundred yards – knock down all the suckers and anthills, clear the rocks and generally level it off, for the aeroplanes were getting bigger these days and needed the extra length of landing ground.

We finished the job in a week, and went up to the homestead for our pay.

'There's one slight problem, lads,' he said. 'You've done a great job, but I don't have any cash to pay you.' We looked crestfallen and he went on quickly, 'No. I have no intention of robbing you, though, so, here, take this key to my store shed and help yourselves to the equivalent value of five pounds each.'

That was fair enough, we thought, and over we went. Now Tom Burrows is one of those impulsive fellows. He raced into the shed, grabbed a 150-lb bag of flour and three packets of Craven A cigarettes, and he was done.

'That's a good five quids worth, eh, Ted?'

I shrugged. You can't teach some people, can you? I moved in slowly, determined not only to be much more selective but to take items which were easier to carry, as we had an 87-mile walk to the nearest watering-hole, the

81

Barrow Creek Pub. So I took a pair of thongs, a torch, a tin of Log Cabin tobacco and cigarette papers, a cigarette lighter, three tins of corned beef and, for good measure, a 7-lb tin of melon and lemon jam.

Away we went, with poor old Burrows quickly regretting the choice of the heavy bag of flour. After much huffing and puffing we completed the 87-mile walk in three and a half hours, and walked breezily into the Barrow Creek Pub, to be greeted by genial Mine Host Jimmy Herreen. No ifs, buts, or how-yergoin, Burrows walked straight up to the bar, hoiked the 150 onto the counter, and said, 'Two foaming pots of beer, please Jimmy.' Jim didn't bat an eyelid. He knew that the barter system was the only way to redress a recession. It's called Keynesian economics. Spend your way out of trouble.

Jim pulled the two pots of beer, and as we started on them with great relish he put Tom's change on the bar. There was a 50-lb bag of flour, a tin of marmalade, and a Geelong Grammar tie. I showed Tom how to do the Windsor knot as we put his tie on for him, and then we finished our beers. Generously, Jimmy shouted next, and then it was my turn.

'Same again, and have one yourself, Jim,' was the order, and Jim complied. I put across the 7-lb tin of jam, and got a bottle of tomato sauce and a tin of wax matches as my change.

We drank our beers and talked of life in general. In walked a dingo trapper, and he threw a bag full of dingo scalps onto the bar. 'I'll shout for the bar,' he exclaimed, which was nice of him.

Jim went over to the corner, counted out eighteen dingo scalps, pulled the three beers for us, had one himself, and then gave the trapper his change. A cake of soap, a deodorant roll-on gizmo, a box of Havana cigars, a jock strap and my former 7-lb tin of melon and lemon jam. Then, for good luck, he threw in a packet of condoms. 'Never know your luck in the big smoke here at Barrow Creek,' said Jim, with that old Herreen twinkle in his eye.

Well, we had a great afternoon, but at about five o'clock there was a terrible bloody commotion out on the verandah. Before we had time to go out to investigate, a bloke came into the bar backwards; he was filthy dirty, and covered in blood. He didn't look to left or right, and then I noticed that he was pulling on a very taut rope. He got inside the bar, still pulling on some unseen thing at the end of the rope. Eventually he got right inside, and suddenly into the bar, on the other end of the rope, came a bloody great sucking pig.

'Can anyone here cash one of Paul Everingham's cheques?' the bloke roared, plaintively.

The Shearers' Bicycle Blowout

THE SHEARERS ALL CAME HURTLING FROM THE SCRUB,
Pedalling fast, and heading for the pub,
The shearers all had bicycles that year,
And they came roaring into town demanding 'Beer!'
Straight into the bar – 'Yee-harrrrr!'

The publican had seen them on the track
And he ran and hid his money out the back,
He knew that if he couldn't cash their cheques,
They'd pour the total value down their necks.
Sure as falling off a log – they'd blow the lot on grog.

84

So the shearers' cheques were placed up on the till
And the shearers started in to drink their fill,
They were singing songs, and dancing merrily,
And the publican rubbed his sweaty hands with glee:
'Come on, drink up men! (*Aside*) I'll get the lot again.'

But after several hours of outback fun,
The leading shearer winked, and said 'Fellers, let's run
A bicycle race, now bikes are all the rage,
Swags up, waterbags full, weight-for-age,
To the cemetery and back? Right, all out on the track.'

The shearers wheeled their bikes out on the track,
And the publican slapped their leader on the back,
He said, 'A bicycle race, what a terrible good idea,
I'll buy the winning rider a butcher of beer.'
He fired off the gun – and they rode – into the sun.

Well, you've never seen such an act in all your life,
The publican ranted and raved and he belted his wife,
For the shearers never came back on that fatal day,
And the publican says that if ever he gets his way,
He'll wring their necks – 'cos they took their bloody
        cheques!

The Good Old Droving Days

NOW, as a drover I know I'm not in Nat Buchanan's league, or Edna Zigenbine's or Matt Savage's, but I did a bit of droving in my youth and I feel privileged to think that I worked for that doyen of 'boss drovers' – the legendary Tom Burrows. You must have heard of him.

I was passing through Queensland, on my way to the Territory, when I met Tom. He had this ongoing contract, taking successive mobs of cattle from Julia Creek right through the middle of Queensland to Cunnamulla, near the

New South Wales border. Have a look at a map, and you'll see how far we had to travel. Well, Tom gave me a job droving with him, and I look back on the four years I had with Tom with great nostalgia – except for one trip!

It used to take us, on average, twelve weeks to walk a mob from Julia Creek to Cunnamulla. You can't do more than ten miles a day, and of course we used to pinch a bit of grass and generally keep our mob in good condition, so we weren't in any hurry. Some of the squatters used to accuse us of stealing their cattle as we went through, but we told them it was natural attrition that reduced their numbers. But I can say that at no time did we ever learn the price of beef in a butcher's shop.

Yes, twelve weeks each trip took. Down, that is. But they were very short of horses in the Cunnamulla district, so at the end of each trip we'd sell our plant of horses. That not only made extra money for us, it enabled us to get back to Julia Creek in only two days, by truck, and then we'd start with the next mob of cattle, with a new plant of horses each time. There are always plenty of good horses around J.C. So twelve weeks down, two days back, trip after trip. It was great experience – except for that one trip!

The droving routine was fairly simple. Nowadays, people find it hard to believe that we used to do the trip with just the two of us, Tom and me – and one of us was driving our old truck. The difference was that we had probably the greatest cattle dog that ever barked, a blue heeler named Blue. Not a very imaginative name for such a clever dog, but there you are. Blue was worth any six men. You didn't need to go on watch at night, no. Blue would 'ring' the cattle at sunset, and they seemed to accept that he was in charge, so they'd settle quietly for the night, and if they were nervous, or looked like 'jumping' on spooky ground, he'd just walk around them a couple of times and they'd quieten down. So the routine was that one of us would ride on horseback, one would drive the truck, and basically Blue would organise the cattle. An incredible dog. Twelve weeks down, two days back. The good old droving days.

Except for that one, dreadful trip. You know that look old bushies get in their eye when they start to get a bit edgy about the booze? Not getting enough, that is? Well, on this particular trip old Tom had a liver like a blanket. He was short-fused, wouldn't talk to me or Blue, and I thought uh-oh, we are going to have problems when we hit Cunnamulla. Sure enough. We delivered the cattle, sold the horses, and straight for the pub headed Burrows. He walked into the bar, pounded his great horny fist on the counter and roared 'Hit me with the Motorbike Special!'

'Pardon?' said the timid little barman.

'Rrrrummm,' said Burrows, and brought a great fist to within a half-inch of the barman's nose.

The barman got the message: perhaps a free drink would help? So he poured Tom a quadruple rum, which went straight down the Burrowsian neck. 'More! More! More!' he was roaring, throwing them down as fast as they were poured, and I was thinking, My God, we'll be here for a month.

So I bided my time, and watched. At about midnight Tom was getting a bit full and had slowed the pace a bit, so I moved in. I grabbed him by the collar of the shirt and the arse of his tweeds, and frog-marched him out to the truck. I chucked him on the back, where I had his swag unrolled, pulled the campsheet over his head, and fortunately he passed out. So I quickly jumped into the cabin and began driving northwards, flat strap, heading for Julia Creek.

I drove all night, and as you can appreciate I was an absolute wreck the next morning. I stopped the truck and had a dingo's breakfast – a leak and a look around – as I watched the sunrise over the western plains. The vision splendid was interrupted by Burrows, who suddenly woke up and began roaring like a scrub bull, 'Where am I? Where am I?'

I wasn't in any great mood, but I thought I'd better humour him so I told him how we'd left the Cunnamulla Pub at midnight and that he'd been a bit the worse for wear, et cetera, cetera, cetera.

Suddenly he began to cry. I've blown it, I thought. What's wrong now? Tom blubbered like a kid. 'I've got a hangover so big you could photograph it,' he said, probably expecting sympathy.

That did it. 'And what about me? I'm the silly bugger who had to look after you all night, and I'm the mug who's going to have to do all the driving to get us back to Julia Creek. Furthermore old feller, remember that we've got to be in J.C. in two days time or we'll lose the contract. You just lie there in your swag. I'll get us through, though I'll have to drive non-stop and flat out for two days and nights.'

Then he sat bolt upright, and looked around. 'Where is he?'

'Where's who?' was my response.

'Blue, of course. Where is he?'

'Look, don't blame me, Tom, he was with you, and he's your dog after all. And you're always saying "One man, one dog". I was too busy looking after you to even think of Blue.'

'Turn around! Straight back to Cunnamulla we go,' said Tom.

I tried to reason with him. 'Tom,' I said, 'if we are not in Julia Creek in two days time we blow the contract. There are drovers galore in Julia Creek who'd love to get that contract. Think about it.'

'What do I do about my dog, son? He's the best cattle dog in the world. I just can't leave him in Cunnamulla. The barmaids eat their young in Cunnamulla, so what would be the fate of the world's smartest canine, eh?'

I was patience itself. 'Tom. Tom, Blue will be alright. He's an intelligent dog, and he'll be sitting at the last place he saw you. Let's head on for Julia Creek now – I'll do the driving – and as soon as we get there you can ring up. Someone at Cunnamulla will have found him. We'll get them to send him up on a truck or a coach, and then he'll be with us for the next mob of cattle. It's as simple as that.'

Oh, no it's not. Would you believe, Tom started to blubber again. 'What in the hell is wrong now?' I demanded. He went through a great miming act. 'I've never used one of them – what do you call them – eau-de-Cologne gadgets in my entire life.'

I exploded. 'Look, I've had enough of this. I'm not going to do the ringing for you. It's your responsibility. He's your dog. I'll get us to Julia Creek, but I'm not doing the telephoning. You are. That's final.'

So I drove flat out and non-stop, and we arrived in Julia Creek after two days and two nights of frenzy. Just in time to take delivery of the cattle. What a relief!

And then I witnessed the spectacle of Tom Burrows, the legend of the outback, the man who can walk cattle across Australia, making his first-ever telephone call. You should have seen it. Perhaps you heard it? He dialled the number and then, when I had instructed him to hold the thing against his ear and talk at the same time, he began to roar.

'Is that the Cunnamulla Hotel?' he bellowed.

'Yes,' said the barman at the other end, 'Cunnamulla Hotel speaking. Who's this calling?' He was probably wondering why Tom used the phone. Why didn't he just shout, his voice was so loud.

'Oh, it's Tom Burrows the drover here,' said Tom, putting on his best lah-de-dah telephone voice. 'Do you remember me, perchance?'

'Yairs, I think I recall you, Mr Burrows. Are you the chap who speaks loudly and drinks rum?'

'Picked me in one, my boy,' said Tom, warming to the electronic age. 'Listen, my good man, I'm ringing about my dog . . . good sort of a dog . . . blue heeler. Answers to the name of "Blue". Would you have seen such a beast around your premises?'

The barman was quick to respond. 'Yes, Mr Burrows, there is a blue dog. He's right here at this very moment. He's been sitting by the fridge for the last couple of days.'

'Right,' said Tom 'put him on the phone, would you, son.'

The barman must have held the phone by the dog's ear, for the next thing was Tom was whistling and calling 'Blue! Bluey! Come here, boy. Come on! Blue!'

And do you know what? Do you know what! Talk about a smart dog. That dog ran to Julia Creek in a day and a half!

All Among the Wool Boys

I HAD A GO at shearing once, and had to tie my sheep up and finish shearing it after lunch – sorry, 'dinner', shearers don't have lunch. I reckon shearers deserve every penny they get. As my old mate, world champion shearer Brian Morrison, says 'It's the only job where you're sweating at 7 a.m. with the frost on the ground outside.' Brian once shore 410 fully grown sheep in 7 hours 48 minutes, using the old 2½-inch blades – the narrow combs, as they've come to be called. It's probably the greatest shearing feat ever achieved, and he lost a stone in weight during that day.

I love to watch the shearing competitions, where points are allocated for fast shearing but subtracted for cuts or improper technique. And it's fascinating to watch the blade shearers, for they hardly make a sound as they undress their sheep. The old song 'Click Go the Shears' is quite inaccurate, really, for the shears didn't 'click' at all – the shearers *drive* the razor-sharp blades through the fleece, mostly having little wooden 'knockers' to prevent the blades from closing and thereby clicking.

The immortal Jacky Howe must have been a marvellous man. It's Jack who's remembered as the best blade-shearer of them all. On 10 October 1892 Jack Howe shore 321 sheep in 7 hours 40 minutes at Alice Downs near Blackall. In the same week Jack shore 1547 sheep, so understandably, when the Alice Downs shed 'cut out' or finished, the shearers all headed for Blackall for a blowout. They stormed into the bar at the Barcoo Hotel, and the publican unwisely turned on free beer for them. He walked over to Jack Howe and congratulated him on his world record, then said, 'Jack, they won't come in here where the shearers drink, but inside in the saloon bar there are three toffs – three graziers – and one of them wants to talk to you about some shearing he wants done.' Jack Howe had a couple of schooners, and then walked into the other bar.

There they were, these three toffs, in their little pork-pie hats, their cutaway duck-arse tweed coats, their white moleskins, their flat-heeled elastic-sided boots, and ties! Ties! Just what you need at Blackall.

They were full of wind and self-importance, and they ignored the common shearer absolutely. So Jack Howe gave a peremptory cough, and they turned haughtily to him.

'Excuse me, gentlemen,' said Jack, 'but I'm Jack Howe the shearer, and I'm told one of you wants to talk about some shearing?'

'Yes, Howe, that's correct,' said one of them, and they resumed their discussion.

Jack was getting a bit fed-up. He coughed again, and they turned to look at this intruder.

'I've just finished shearing at Alice Downs, so I can shear for you next week if that suits you.'

'Very well, Howe, next week. You may go now.'

'But hang on, I'll need to have some idea how long it will take me. How many sheep do you have altogether?'

The cockies were getting a bit churlish about this upstart. 'Don't worry about numbers, Howe' said the silvertail, 'I have seventy sheep.'

'And tell me,' Jack responded, 'what are their names?'

It was during the Korean War that wool reached the amazing price of one pound sterling for one pound weight of wool. It was a bit like the four-minute mile: everybody said it couldn't happen. But it did.

Australia to this day has a lot of absentee landlords, so in 1953 there was rejoicing among the so-called gentry in England as they scored the benefits of this incredible price increase. The manager of a big station in the Riverina sent a telegram to his boss in London, as follows:

LORD FOTHERINGHAM
PICCADILLY CLUB
LONDON UK

PLEASED TO INFORM YOU WOOL TODAY REACHED
THE INCREDIBLE PRICE OF ONE POUND STERLING

PER POUND WEIGHT. SHEARING JUST COMPLETED
AND YOU WILL UNDOUBTEDLY REAP GREAT
BENEFIT FROM THIS WONDERFUL PRICE INCREASE.
MANAGER

When the telegram arrived Lord Fotheringham was
sipping a port, actually. Thrilled with the news, he called
for an amanuensis, and sent this reply:

MANAGER
LACHLAN DOWNS
THE RIVERINA
AUSTRALIA

WONDERFUL NEWS. SUGGEST TAKE FULL
ADVANTAGE THIS SITUATION. START SHEARING
AGAIN IMMEDIATELY.   FOTHERINGHAM

It's strange but true that in Australia, the Land of the
Golden Fleece, there are many people who've never seen
a live sheep, for there aren't many sheep in the Top End,
the country north of the Tropic of Capricorn. Tommy
Burrows was in this category when he was a young fellow.
He'd been born on the Atherton Tableland, and worked as
a ringer on the big cattle stations in the Gulf Country.

When he was about eighteen, Tom took a trip to
Sydney. For reasons I must not disclose he ran out of
cash, so he thought: 'It's a bit of a problem, but I'll take a
job for a bit, get a few bob together, and then head back
up north. Tom went to an employment agency, and was
thrilled as he walked in the door, for there was a big sign
saying 'Wanted. Station-hands.' Well, thought Tom, it's
my lucky day. He walked up to the counter.

'Yes?' said the girl.

'Reckon I'm yer man,' said Tom, pointing at the sign. 'The name's Thomas Anzac Burrows, and I'm a station-hand.'

'Great!' said the girl, and she signed him up to work on a station out west of Wagga Wagga, in the Riverina. She didn't think to mention to Tom that it was a sheep station, so she had no knowledge that Tom had never seen a sheep in his life.

She gave Tom a train ticket, and out west he went. He got off the train at a little siding, expecting to be met by a big, tough cattleman, the sort of employer he'd had in the Gulf. To his surprise there was this joker in a little how's-yer-fancy hat. He told Tom that he was the owner of the station, and piled him into an air-conditioned Mercedes, if you don't mind.

As they drove out to the station Tom was looking for cattle – didn't see any, but he made no comment. But when they got a bit closer to the station the boss said, 'Look over there Tom, there's the shed, and the drafting yards.' Tom didn't know what he was supposed to reply, so he said nothing. But he'd still seen no cattle. Eventually they stopped and got out of the car. Tom had a look around, and then he saw these strange little black things, like currants, all over the ground.

'Excuse me boss' he said, 'I don't want to sound like an ignoramus on my first day, but what are those little round black things?'

The boss took a shrewd look at Thomas. 'Oh, those things?' he said slowly, 'We call those things "Get-Smart Pills".'

'Is that so?' replied Tom.

'Yes,' said the boss. 'Would you like to try one, Tom?'

Anxious to make a good impression, Tom said, 'Why

not? When in Rome, do as the Romans do. Hit me with a Get-Smart Pill.'

The boss stooped, picked one off the ground, and said 'Open up!' Tom opened his gob, the boss dropped the G.S.P. in his mouth, and Tom began chewing, stoically. After a moment he said, frowning, 'Doesn't seem to be doing much for me.'

The boss said, 'Maybe you Top End blokes need a double dose. Try another one.'

Tom himself picked one from the ground, flicked it high into the air, and deftly caught it in his mouth. He gave it a good, salivarous chew, then turned to the boss and said, 'You know what, boss? It tastes a bit like shit.'

'See!' said the boss, 'You're getting smart already!'

Shim
Reen

D ID YOU KNOW Jimmy Herreen by any chance? What a man! Died a while back, Jim, and the world's a poorer place altogether. I still get a bit depressed from time to time, and then I think of the funny things that always seemed to happen around him and I cheer up. Jim was a man of many parts, a great lover of the important things in life, like women and rum. He was a wonderful horseman, and he ran a team of packhorses on the Kokoda Trail during the Second World War. After the war he came back to the Territory and finished up on the Hatches

Creek wolfram field, among other ventures into the mining game. At Hatches Creek Jimmy had an old Aboriginal chap named Friday working as his offsider, and Friday used to call him Shim Reen.

Well, Jimmy was due for his holidays, so he left Friday in charge of the claim and off he went to Adelaide to the Cup. A couple of days before he was due to return to the Territory, Jim went to an army disposals sale and he bought a plunger detonator – you know, those things they have in the cowboy pictures when they're going to blow up the bridge. You set the charge, press the plunger and kerboom! Jim loaded this gadget onto his truck and drove north, through Alice Springs and then back out to Hatches Creek. There was Friday, waiting for him, thrilled to bits at his boss's return.

The old bloke ran his eye over the load on the back of the truck, and he spotted this new device. 'What that?' he queried.

'That, Friday, is a plunger detonator,' said Jimmy, 'and you and I are going to let off the greatest explosion Hatches Creek has ever seen.' Friday was duly impressed, and watched as Jim took the plunger off the truck and set it up on a concrete block at the top of the mine shaft. His eyes opened wide as Jim next took twenty sticks of gelignite from a box and climbed down into the bottom of the mine shaft. There, he set the charge. Detonators, fuses, right, ready to go. Up the ladder, out of the shaft came Jim, with Friday watching his every move. Jim connected the terminals on the plunger, and then turned to his old companion.

'Now, I'll tell you what I want you to do, Friday,' said Jim. 'I'm going to hide in the tent, so I can make a dramatic entry. I want you to go right around the field, and get every single bloke over here for the big explosion. But whatever you do, don't tell them what's going on. Just tell them that Jimmy Herreen's got a big surprise for them. OK?'

'Right, Shim,' said the old bloke, and away he went. This was all Friday needed to boost his stocks a bit, so he squared the shoulders and shouted to all and sundry. 'Right, you blokes, get over here right away. Come on allabout! Shim Reen got a big surprise for you feller. Come on. Straight away.'

Over they came, to Jimmy's camp – about two hundred curious miners. Jim was nowhere to be seen. Friday noted with satisfaction that they were all impressed with the new device, but none of them seemed to know what it was.

'Shentlemen,' said Friday, 'you friend and mine. Presenting Shim Reen!'

Out bounded Jimmy, and wasted no time. Straight to the plunger he went. 'Stand back, please gentlemen,' he said, and they all gave him room. He grabbed the plunger handles and pressed, and . . . nothing happened. There was a guffaw or two. Friday scowled, and Jim apologised.

'Sorry, chaps, it's my first go. I must have overlooked something.' With that he walked over to the mine shaft and began to climb down the ladder. 'Won't be a moment,' he called as he disappeared down the shaft.

Very carefully he descended the ladder, and gingerly he checked the charge. Dynamite, OK. Detonators, fuses, all in place, all tight. Ready to fire. Back up the ladder, and every eye was on him.

'She'll work this time, I promise you,' said Jim, as he walked over to the plunger. He checked the terminals were tight, then he grabbed the handles and was just about to press the plunger.

'Stop! Stop, Shim!' said Friday.

Jim was puzzled. 'What?' said Jim.

'Stop, Shim. No good. He still buggered, that thing.' Friday pointed to the offending plunger.

Jim put his hands on his hips. 'And what would you bloody well know about things?' he asked the old man.

'Well,' explained Friday, 'I'm pushim couple o' times while you down the hole!'

Jimmy always insisted that was the reason he finished up buying the Barrow Creek Pub. He said that he looked meaningfully at the axe, and Friday got the message and took off like a fart from a goose. In the aftermath Jim started to shake, and he reckoned there was only one cure for that – rum. So he got in the truck and bounced over the hundred miles across country to the Barrow Creek Pub. After a couple of rums the shakes stopped. After a couple of weeks on the rum he was as happy as a dog with two dicks, so he decided he'd had enough of mining. He took out his cheque book, wrote out a cheque, and bought the pub.

The
Rules of
the Bush

I RECKON I could write a book about Jim Herreen, so I hope you don't mind if I go on about him a bit longer.

He said to me one day, 'Ted,' he said, 'you know how I always observe the time-honoured conventions of the bush?'

I must have looked typically dumb at his use of long words.

'The Rules of the Bush,' he explained.

'Oh yes, got you, Jim.' I nodded.

He expanded. 'You know how we always say "Never camp in the dry bed of a creek", don't we?'

'That's right,' I said. 'I've heard you say it a hundred times.'

'Well,' he went on, 'I have told you, and every other person I know, the reason for that. The creek may be dry and warm and sheltered on a cold windy night, but you never know what the weather's doing say fifty miles away, do you? There might be a sudden storm, a flash flood, and the creek can come rushing down on you, while it hasn't rained a drop where you're camped. There have been quite a few people drowned that way.'

I nodded, and waited for him to continue.

'About ten days ago, I was coming in from a prospecting trip out bush. It was absolutely freezing, and it came time to camp. Here was this nice, sheltered creek bed. Nobody forced me to do it. It's my own bloody fault. I decided that rather than camp up on the bank and put up with the icy wind and the prospect of a frost I parked my truck under a tree, and took my swag and tucker box down into the dry, sandy creek bed. Yes, as I thought, it was relatively protected – out of the wind, and the sand warm and soft. A perfect spot to camp. And not a cloud in the sky. There's the old Southern Cross, and Pegasus, and the Milky Way. Nothing in the world matches a night under the Australian stars. To mark the occasion, I thought I should do something special. I unrolled my swag neatly on the sand, and then I made a little fire. While I was waiting for the coals to form I unscabbed a brand-new 40 oz. bottle of Bundaberg Rum. I had a couple of nips of rum from my pannikin, and then I made a couple of johnny-cakes, which I had with a couple of slices of salt beef, washed down, of course, by another Bundaberg. Peace and contentment pervaded the bush. I sat there for a while, relaxed, and then I got ready for bed. I stripped down to my jocks, took out the old false teeth, and placed them on the top of the tucker box, alongside the bottle of rum. Then I hopped into the swag for one of the greatest sleeps of my life . . .

'And then, at about 3 a.m., I heard it! The creek was coming down! The roar of the water. Here she comes! I bounded out of the swag, got my bearings and thought, "Run, run for your life, Jim." I had a split second to spare, enough time to grab just one thing as I ran. Only half awake, I remember thinking, "The choppers or the rum. What'll it be?"'

'And what did you go for, Jim?' I asked.

'Well,' he said, stoically, 'me dental appointment's next Thursday!'

A postscript to the story is that the next time Jim passed that creek he had a bit of a search for his old teeth, and found them, half a mile downstream, under a great cow turd!

★ ★ ★ ★ ★

Jim Herreen was a great man for profundities. No, not profanities, profundities. He came up to me one day, seemingly serious for a change, and said, 'You know, Ted, you *can* kiss an emu on the arse, but you've got to be moving real fast at the time!'

Bush
Telegraph

THE ROYAL FLYING DOCTOR SERVICE is a wonderful institution, founded of course by John Flynn and
incorporating aeroplanes and wireless to provide
'a mantle of safety for the outback'.

For many years before telephones became common,
the R.F.D.S. radio network was the only means whereby
people in the bush had any outside contact. After the
medical sessions were completed, the operator at the base
would call for 'general traffic'. There would be bedlam for a
moment or two as the various stations announced their
call-signs and they were listed in order as the operator

recognised them. Naturally those with the strongest signal were on the top of the list for traffic, a fact of life very irksome to 'the battlers' – those furthest from town. One bloke who used to get very frustrated was a cattleman named Bill Lavington, who lived on a station named Kurrundi, east of Barrow Creek and Wauchope, and about five hundred miles from the Alice Springs R.F.D.S. base.

You've got to remember that the R.F.D.S. was founded by 'Flynn of the Inland' and that John Flynn was a Presbyterian clergyman. So the protocol has always been that no unseemly language is tolerated, and there is no mention made of either strong drink or gambling. All sorts of euphemisms have been used over the years, and bets on the races are usually sent in the most obscure language – with everybody listening in, of course, as some of the bushies are good judges of horseflesh. Cartons of beer are usually called 'loaves of bread' or somesuch. One recipient of a telegram for fifty loaves of bread sent just that – to the joy of the drilling team out in the bush whose skins were cracking after three months of temperance.

Bill Lavington spent a lot of time in the stock camp, and his only radio was a small portable set with, naturally, a fairly weak signal. So time after time Bill would be last on the list, and he would have to wait sometimes an hour listening to all the richer people close to town sending telegrams to their stockbrokers, etc. You can imagine Bill sitting on the ground fuming, the little set crackling beside him, a piece of fencing wire for an aerial, cattle in hand, and having to wait. One day George Brown, the operator in Alice, called for general traffic. In they came, the rich and powerful, with their strong signals, and once again Bill Lavington was last on the list with his plaintive signal. 'Eight Sugar Easy X-Ray, 8 S.E.X., Eight Sugar Easy X-Ray.' George reeled off the signals of those who would take precedence over Bill, and said, 'Last on the list I have Eight Sierra Easy X-Ray, Kurrundi. That's "S" for Sierra, not Sugar.'

The telegrams went on, and on, and on. Eventually it was Bill's turn. George Brown said, 'And now, Eight Sierra Easy X-Ray, it's over to you for traffic. Good morning, Bill.'

'Morning, George,' came the reply. 'One telegram, George, how do you read? Over.'

'Faint, as usual, Bill, but give it a try.'

'Right George, one telegram. Address: Elder Smith Alice Springs. Text: PLEASE SEND THREE LARGE BAGS FLOUR, ONE BY SEVENTY POUND BAG SUGAR, TEN POUNDS TEA, ONE CARTON PLUM JAM, THREE PAIRS FENCING PLIERS, TWENTY BUNDLES STAR PICKETS, FIVE ROLLS BARBED WIRE, ONE CARTON ABORIGINAL TOBACCO, TWO PAIR R.M. WILLIAMS BOOTS SIZE ELEVEN. And George, could you ask Elders to send me out some grog.'

The dreaded four-letter word. Grog. Over John Flynn's sacred airwaves.

Somewhat tongue-in-cheek George Brown came back. 'Bill, I got a fair bit of that. Let's see, flour, sugar, tea, jam, pliers, droppers, barbed wire, tobacco, Williams boots size eleven. But I didn't quite catch that last item. Could you say again? Over.'

'Grog!' roared Bill in reply. 'Tell them to send me some grog.'

'Still not reading you, Bill,' said George. 'Try again.'

Bill was getting mad. 'Grog!' came the blood-curdling roar.

Everybody in the bush was now listening, but George Brown, who liked a joke, wasn't going to give in too easily. 'Sorry, Bill, I'm afraid you're going to have to give it to me a letter at a time – and use the air traffic alphabet please.'

'How do you mean?' retorted Bill.

'You know, A equals Alpha, B equals Bravo, et cetera.
And give it to me slowly, and as distinctly as possible
please.'

'Right, here we go,' responded Bill. 'Let's see now.
Grog. G for Jesus, R for Arsehole, O for 'Opeless and G
for Jesus you stupid bastard. Tell them to send me some
GROG! Over.'

The Parragundy Stiffener

WAY OUT AT PARRAGUNDY, WHERE THE PAROO RIVER
    RUNS,
The bushies had survived for years on rum and Biggins
    buns.
But the publican named Paddy got the locals feeling frisky,
When he began to serve a drink called Parragundy
    Whiskey.

The recipe was famous, he'd learnt it from his Dad,
Who'd come out to Australia as an Irish convict lad,

Scoop the innards from a pumpkin, and pour the metho in
With raisins and some neatsfoot oil, and watch the fun
    begin.

When the brew had all fermented, and the juice had
    simmered down,
He'd try it on the native tribe who lived on the edge of
    town.
They'd 'coo-ee' and they'd 'yackai' and they'd dance
    around the scrub,
And if they survived 'til morning, he'd serve it in the pub.

But Christmas came a scorching, and the tribe could not
    be found,
And then a thirsty mob of bushies came roaring in to town,
Their livers were like blankets, and their hides were
    cracking, too,
But when Paddy wouldn't serve a drink, they all stacked
    on a blue.

Old Paddy said, 'Now listen, lads, I'd like a bit of shoosh,
I tink the brew's too potent, but the blacks have all gone
    bush.
It wouldn't be right to serve you, I tink you'll all agree,
So how's about some Biggins buns, and a nice hot cup of
    tea?'

'Come on, you Irish bastard, and serve us all a drink,
If the keg can hold it we can, no matter what you "tink".'
So Paddy broached the caskets, and he started in to pour,
And the brew was named 'the Stiffener' from that day to
    evermore.

Epitaph
Six thirsty men are buried where the Paroo River runs,
Above their heads, for tombstones, are six king-sized
    Biggins buns.
It only goes to show, me lads, it's always somewhat risky
To take a lethal overdose of Parragundy Whiskey.

News Headlines

THE NEWSPAPER in Alice Springs is called the *Centralian Advocate*, and one of its best-known editors was a bloke named Bob Watt. Not Bob Who, Bob Watt. Bob's now transferred to Darwin, working on the *Northern Territory News*, and it's Darwin's gain and Alice's loss.

Prior to his departure for Darwin Bob was engaged in a fairly hectic round of farewells. He was on his way one day to visit a mate who lived out of town a bit, driving along, all serene, when suddenly he stopped the car and began running towards a paddock. There in the paddock he had spotted a huge Brahman bull, a great, mean-looking monster with gleaming white horns, fierce red blood-shot eyes, a great gristly hump, balls like Paroo mailbags, and a brass ring through its nose. This bull was pawing the ground, obviously about to charge someone, or something, and eagle-eyed Bob Watt discerned that the object of the bull's displeasure was a tiny, defenceless little five-year-old girl, who was standing there petrified.

'I must save the child, I must save the child,' Bob thought, as he ran towards the paddock. But there was one big problem. Between Bob and the act was a netting and barbed-wire fence – six foot two, impenetrable. 'Well,' thought Bob quickly, 'there's only one thing for it. I'm going to have to try out that new-fangled high jump, the Fosbury Flop, but I must save the child.'

He'd seen the Fosbury Flop on TV a few times, and it looked straightforward enough. You just ran in, flipped yourself over the bar backwards, arched your back, kicked your legs over, and did a backward roll as you hit the other side. Easy. So in he ran.

But you know how sometimes your legs won't take you where your brain wants you to go? The occasion was just too big for Bob. He got into take-off position, with one foot raised and his legs poised for the spring, but he couldn't get off the ground. It was as though he were frozen on the spot. Couldn't move a muscle.

Then the bull began to charge! It pawed the ground viciously, then began to thunder down the paddock when suddenly, out of the blue, came this figure – a seventeen-year-old youth – riding into view on a pushbike. Well, the young fellow spotted what was happening and he didn't hesitate. He threw down his bicycle, hurdled that fence if

you don't mind – losing nothing whatsoever in the process, I might add – and then raced towards the child. Just as the bull was about to knock the little girl to smithereens, this intrepid youth grabbed the bull by the ring in its nose, flipped it deftly off balance, and then threw the bull on its side. It had to be seen to be believed. Then, like lightning, he took a knife from its sheath on his belt, slit the bull's throat, and it's dead. Four legs twitching in the air. Dead! And the little girl was saved.

At that point, Bob Watt's legs started to function again and, of course, he was committed to the high jump – the dreaded Fosbury Flop. Over the fence he went, crashing to the ground on the other side, did his backward roll and came up covered in dust and bindy-eyes, totally disoriented. When he regained his composure a bit, Bob staggered out into the middle of the paddock, where all the action had taken place without him. He walked up to the young chap with his hand extended. 'Young man!' he said. 'Young man, that was the bravest deed I have ever seen in my life. I know just how brave you were, son, because I witnessed the same set of circumstances, but my unworthy legs just wouldn't take me out there. Yet you ... you just didn't hesitate.' Bob looked admiringly at the lad. And then the professional took over. 'Son, I'm the editor of the local newspaper, the *Advocate*, and I'd like to do a feature story on you for Friday's edition. I can see it now, the full front page, photographs, and furthermore my boy, I'm going to recommend you for the highest bravery award in the land.'

The boy stood there, modest, unassuming, a little embarrassed by it all, but Bob hadn't finished.

'No, my boy, the world will know how you leapt off your bicycle, cleared the fence, killed this dreadful monster and saved (he patted the little girl's head) ... saved this little child's life. Son, I'd like to shake your hand (and he did, vigorously) because I want to put on record the opinion that what you just did was arguably the bravest deed ever performed by a young Australian.'

The youth gave a little smile. 'Funnily enough,' he responded, 'I'm not, as a matter of fact, an Australian. I'm just out here from England, actually, having a bit of colonial experience. Jolly topping, what?'

Bob reeled backwards. And do you know what the headline was in the *Advocate*?

POMMY BASTARD MURDERS CHILD'S PET!

The Perils of Outback Travel

NOW, don't ever let anyone tell you that outback travel is a pushover nowadays. Yes, I'll acknowledge that with all the bitumen roads, and better motor cars, and roadhouses and things like that, it is easier, but you should never underestimate the harshness of this country if you're travelling in the more remote regions. Every year you seem to hear of somebody perishing, simply because they panicked in the bush. Take lots of food and water, enough spare parts, and if you break down *never* leave your vehicle. I'm sure Jack Absolom would agree with me.

Among this collection of mostly 'lighter' tales, I'd like to include a very sad little story which goes back to 1927. There was a married couple travelling from Marree to Birdsville, up the dreaded Birdsville Track. It's a tricky road nowadays, but in 1927 it was just a two-wheel track through the sandhills, and only about one vehicle a month traversed it. Pretty lonely, dangerous stuff.

The couple were driving in an old A-model Ford, a utility loaded up with their gear and supplies. It was the middle of summer, especially dangerous, with temperatures approaching 113°F every day. Well, they were half way along the Track when they broke an axle. Serious, to say the least. But they had one thing in their favour. They were locals, both born in the bush, good at improvising, and they knew the one important rule: no matter how much you're tempted, *never* leave your vehicle. They'd heard of the many people who'd broken down, left their vehicles and gone looking for homesteads, bores, God knows what, and of course within an hour they'd stripped off their clothes, walked round and round in circles, and perished. No, this couple knew that, come what may, they must stay with the truck.

They tried to fix the broken axle, but to no avail. They tried every trick they knew, but with no luck. A week went by, and of course by this time they'd used all their water. The water in the waterbag was gone, the water in the canteen they always carried for emergencies – gone. Even the water in the radiator – drained out and used. Peril was staring them in the face.

The husband, a tough and resolute bushman, went and sat in the meagre shade afforded by a little gidgee bush.

After a while he came back to his wife, and said, 'Isn't it strange? I sat there, and my whole life seemed to flash past me, as though on some sort of a screen. And . . . I . . . well, dear, I reflected on our, what, twenty years of . . . well, happiness if you like.'

The wife wiped a little tear from her eye. 'Yes, it's been good, hasn't it. The normal ups-and-downs, I guess, but . . . yes, a very happy married life.' She knew what he was getting at.

'I was thinking, dear,' said the man, 'that we could well perish here, and I think it's better to face up to facts like that.' The wife nodded, and said nothing.

The husband brightened a little. 'Why don't we, while all our faculties are still in place, why don't we do something on a . . . symbolic level . . . to mark the fact that we've had a good life together?' He had an idea. 'Why don't we check through the tuckerbox, see if we can find some little morsel of food to share on a . . . well, a ritual basis.'

'A bit like communion?' said the wife.

'Well, I guess so,' he answered.

'What a beautiful thought,' she said, and began to rummage around in the tucker box. There, to her delight, she found a little calico bag with a small amount of self-raising flour in it. Just the thing! 'Why don't we make a little damper, a little unleavened loaf, and share it, in the full knowledge that it could be our last meal together?'

'A great idea,' he said, and went to get the little dish they always used to make damper. She quickly emptied the flour into the dish. But then, she stopped, dismayed. 'Not such a good idea,' she said. 'To make a damper we need water, and we don't have any.'

'Oh, God,' said the husband, 'of course we don't have any water. We've even used the water from the radiator.

123

Oh well, never mind, it was a good idea. A lovely idea.'

The wife gave him a strange look. 'I'll tell you what to do,' she said slowly, 'piss in it.'

'What!' he roared, shocked beyond belief. 'Oh, darling, how could you suggest such a thing.'

She was insistent. 'Darling,' she said, 'there is nobody within two hundred miles of us in any given direction. Nobody will see you, and it's not going to worry me. I've been married to you for over twenty years. Piss in it!'

The husband shrugged. 'Well, if it doesn't worry you, it doesn't worry me.' So he positioned himself above the dish containing the flour, and he strained and groaned and struggled for a full minute before he gave up.

'Sorry, darling, but I guess I'm so dehydrated I can't raise a single drop. Not a drop.'

'Well, maybe I can help, dear. I'll have a go,' said the wife, and approached the dish. She dropped her nickers, squatted over the dish, and . . . would you believe it . . . she farted, and blew all the flour away!

So it's not all laughs in the bush, is it?

PS You know, I wasn't sure how to 'title' this story. I thought at the outset I might call it 'Gone with the Wind', but I seem to think someone else has used that title already.

The Reluctant Saddler

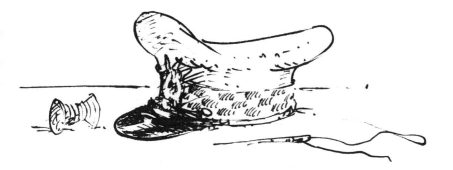

BIDDY AND TOM had been married for about ten years. Well, not really married, but out at Borroloola nobody worries about bits of paper so it didn't make any difference. Not until that smart young copper was posted to the Loo.

He was going to clean the place up, he said. He'd learnt at the police academy that you shouldn't allow any sort of a sloppy set-up, so he saw the Loo as a tremendous challenge. The blacks for one thing: he'd smarten them up. A bit of military-style discipline would be good for them.

He'd have them growing their own vegetables and wearing clean clothes at all times. That corroboree nonsense would cease, and there'd be no more fraternising with those no-hoper white blokes who came in for the wet season.

You can imagine what a stir this caused. Old Harry Thompson had been the walloper at the Loo for the previous fifteen years and he'd fitted in perfectly. Sired a couple of yellerfellers and could fight and drink rum with the best of them. He made the odd arrest when the police station needed repairs or painting, and he used to put on a good show when the Commissioner came around every two years. He'd get old Sam Turner and Albert Morcom to dress up as prisoners and they'd regale the Commissioner with tales about how tough old Thommo was.

This new joker's name was Lester. Richard Lester. Not Dick: Richard. The locals tested him out in all the usual ways, but to no avail. He didn't drink, thank you, and thought smoking was a weakness. Had no interest in cards and threatened to lock up anyone who organised a two-up game. The final blow to the locals' hopes came when they planted Bessie, old Tiger's daughter, in the copper's bed. Not only did he knock her back, but he marched her down to Tiger's camp and said the old bloke would be charged the following morning with contributing to the delinquency of a minor. Tiger was impressed by the formal language even though he didn't understand a word, but the local death adders were shattered. How can we bring him down to size if he's not human?

Ignorance is bliss, and Tom rode in from the Tableland at the start of the wet season. Biddy rode behind him on a donkey. They had two packhorses and Tom had a big cheque. He'd been at Anthony's Lagoon right through the dry season and he'd fitted in a bit of yard-building as well as doing up all the saddles. He was a delight to watch at the

126

saddlery game, definitely the best craftsman in the back country.

'You're Mr Tom Lee, I believe?' said Constable Richard Lester the next day at the store.

'That's right, mate.'

'Well, Mr Lee, I hear you're something of a saddler?'

'So they say.'

'It so happens, Mr Lee, that the police saddles haven't been done up for several years and they're in a disgraceful condition.'

'Oh?'

The upshot of this was that the copper wanted all the saddles counterlined, all packs done up, new greenhide ropes, new hobbles, the lot. He'd cleared it with Darwin and was in a position to offer Tom fifty bob a week for up to six weeks to take on the contract.

Tommy didn't like coppers at the best of times, but he had a great laugh at this impudent young twit. Gave him a piece of his mind, too.

'Do you think I'd work for the police?' he said. 'What would the mob think of me? And fifty bloody bob a week! Mate, I never work during the wet season in any case, but as it happens I've got a cheque for three hundred and eighty quid in my kick, and me and the mob are going to get into the greatest bender since old Jensen's wake. But first of all me and the missus is goin' up to the Landing for a spot of fishing. So my advice to you mate is to fix your own bloody saddles, and jam your fifty bob up your dinger.'

The cop was furious. He became aware that the locals were sniggering at him, and he knew from police academy that this was intolerable. What was it their lecturer had told them? You must at all times hold the upper hand and take the initiative.

'Duncan,' he said to the tracker, 'that fellow Tom Lee.

He says that he and his wife are going up to the Landing for fishing. But I've never seen anyone around who could be Mrs Lee. Where is she? What does she look like?'

'Oh, Tommy wife there alright,' said Duncan, pointing with his chin towards the river. 'She name Biddy. She my really sister,' he added proudly.

'You mean that Lee's married to an Aboriginal!' exclaimed Constable Richard Lester.

'Well, him not really married white feller fashion,' replied the ingenuous Duncan, 'but Tommy bin squarim me three bag of flour, one rifle and one packsaddle so me bin marryim for Biddy.'

If Tom had known what was coming he'd have headed east from the Landing instead of returning to the Loo. But he and Biddy had caught eight catties, two mangrove schnapper and a beautiful barra, about fifteen pounds, so he thought he'd head back and start on the rum with Roger and Andy. Biddy could cook them a few fish and then go off with the women for a couple of days.

Odd. There was the new copper waiting at his camp. As Tom tied up the canoe and Biddy began to carry the fish to the camp Constable Lester strode to the water's edge.

'Thomas Lee,' he sprouts, 'I'm placing you under arrest on a charge of cohabiting with a female Aboriginal, and I must warn you that anything you say may be taken down and used as evidence against you.'

The Loo had never seen such a day. A visiting magistrate from Darwin heaved and panted in the steamy heat that only Borroloola can turn on. The locals all turned up and they were really savage. Their livers were like blankets, and their hides were cracking: they'd all been looking forward to Tom's blowout, but the copper had confiscated his cheque.

'Thomas Lee,' intoned the prosecutor, 'you stand charged that on the seventeenth day of October you did cohabit with a female Aboriginal named Biddy Noongali without the permission in writing of the Chief Protector of Aboriginals, contrary to section forty-seven of the Aboriginals Ordinance 1918–1923. How do you plead, guilty or not guilty?'

Tommy never had a chance. He nodded the skull to the charge and Constable Richard Lester, police constable stationed at Borroloola, rose to outline 'the facts in this case, Your Worship.' Tom was asked if he had anything to say, but he limited himself to muttering that the country was getting too civilised. The magistrate, who was anxious to wind up this case and get into a bit of serious drinking, wiped his dripping forehead and announced in sombre tones that he had no alternative in this matter but to impose the mandatory sentence of six months hard labour. There was a gasp from the gallery, or rather the mango tree under which all the locals were squatting. Six months! That meant Tommy's cheque would be out of circulation until March. She'd be a dangerous wet season this year. Lock up all the razors, as they say.

Worse was to follow. The magistrate asked whether Tom shouldn't go to Fannie Bay to do his sixer, but Constable Lester said no Your Worship that won't be necessary we have adequate facilities here at Borroloola for a term of imprisonment of this kind thank you Constable silence all stand Borroloola Police Court stands adjourned *sine die*.

That was twenty years ago, and Tommy Lee hasn't been back to Borroloola. He did his stretch and he did it hard, and on the day he was released he shot through. Biddy joined him at the Landing. They headed due east this time and finished up on a station near Normanton, I believe.

And Constable Lester? Senior Constable Lester if you don't mind. He got a gong as a result of the Commissioner's visit, the principal reason for the promotion being the excellent condition of all the police plant and equipment, in particular the saddlery, which had been done up by unskilled prison labour under the close personal supervision of Constable Lester himself. He seems to me, reported the Commissioner, a very promising young officer, bound to go a long way in the force if he can continue to offer such excellent rehabilitative projects for prisoners, who must surely derive considerable benefit and enjoyment from imaginative training of this type.

Original Australian Humour

ANYBODY WHO, like me, has had the good fortune to spend a lot of time with Aboriginal people in the bush, will tell you that the predominant thing in their lives is laughter. I think it's something of a pity that we don't realise just how much of Aboriginal humour and philosophy affects the Australian ethos. I just wish everybody could have the experiences I have had.

A lot of Aboriginal humour derives from the fact that they, generally, are so incredibly logical and non-Aboriginals aren't, and this often turns 'unfunny' things into 'funny' things.

Take an old bloke like Jockey Bundubundu. He's a Gunabidji, from the Liverpool River in Arnhem Land. He's an incredible bushman, one of the greatest I've ever seen – one of those blokes who'll teach you something every five minutes if you're wanting to learn. He and I had many a laugh shooting crocodiles in his country in the fifties, when I was posted to Arnhem Land to help set up a station called Maningrida. About a year after I had been posted back to Darwin, Jockey came into town for a visit. He'd been to Darwin before, so was not unfamiliar with town life. It was the middle of the wet season, and I was giving him a lift into town from the Bagot Reserve. I was driving a Land Rover with a covered canvas back, and the rain was really pelting down and I couldn't see the rear-vision mirror on the passenger's side. I came to a Stop sign where the Stuart Highway met the old 'American' road at Parap, and I had to give way at what was an upside-down V situation. So I stopped. Jockey was sitting alongside me, looking straight ahead. 'Any car coming?' I said, in what I felt was the language he would have used. He slowly turned his head, looked searchingly back along the road with his all-observant bushman's eyes, then turned back to me and said, 'No'. I put the car into gear and slowly started to move. Without any panic Jockey said to me, as I got up a bit of speed, 'Only one truck!'

And there was a dear old bloke named Bill Stanner, Professor Bill Stanner actually, an anthropologist who did a lot of memorable research in the Territory and delighted to tell stories against himself about his experiences among Aboriginals. Prof was an Australian, but he had studied at Oxford and he spoke with a fairly toffy voice. He was a round, koala-like figure, and usually puffed on his very aromatic pipe as he told his yarns over a nice bottle of red.

'When I was working on the Daly,' he said one night, 'I engaged an old Aboriginal chap named Paddy to be my guide and mentor. Well, I was driving one day from the Daly to Port Keats, along a bush track of course, and Paddy was sitting alongside me in the passenger's seat of my truck. The old chap fell fast asleep. So I was driving along, at peace with the world and thinking about my various research projects, when I came to this amazing stretch of country. On the left-hand side of the road there were thousands, literally thousands, of little ant-hills all about three feet tall, and yet on the right-hand side not a single one. It was like this for several miles, and finally my curiosity got the better of me. I reached across and shook the old man's arm. "Paddy," I called, "Paddy, wake up!" The old man was in the deepest of sleeps. "What! What wrong?" he shouted, and then gradually realised that I had woken him. "What wrong?" he repeated. "Paddy," I said, apologetically, "I'm sorry to wake you, old chap, but I'm fascinated by this stretch of country we're passing through. How is it that on that side of the road there are thousands of ant-hills, and yet on the other side of the road not a single one?" The old bloke looked from side to side, slowly, thought for a bit, then had another look, left-hand side, furrowed brow, right-hand side, thought a bit more. And then very slowly, pointing from side to side to reinforce the statement, he said, "Well, this side, gottim plenty hants . . . and that side, gottim no hants." And the old bastard went straight back to sleep!'

One day I was at a place called Milikapiti (Snake Bay) on Melville Island. Sitting down on the beach was old Navy Paddy, a very funny old bloke. He had a newspaper on his lap, but it was upside down. I said to him, 'I didn't know you could read, old feller?' He said, 'I can't read, but (he tapped the newspaper knowingly) I still know what they're saying about us blackfellers.'

Another time I was shooting crocs with a bloke named Harry Mulumbuk, on the Blyth River. Nowadays crocodiles are protected and I have mixed feelings about the way we used to hunt them, but I was a patrol officer at the time and helping Aboriginals to hunt and sell the skins, for this was the only means whereby people in Arnhem Land could get any money. Even if there had been work Aborigines were only paid ten shillings a week, whereas some of the blokes I was working with, who were expert bushmen, could earn twenty pounds from just a medium-sized skin – the price at the time was a pound per inch measured across the belly, and we more often than not could get five crocs a night. So it was the financial mainstay of Arnhem Land, and we only took big male crocs usually.

Anyway, back to Harry Mulumbuk. We were up this very narrow, mangrove-lined creek and we spotted the eyes of this quite big – about 14 feet long – croc in the spotlight. We were in a dugout canoe, about twelve feet long, with about six inches of freeboard and not very stable. When you hunt a croc you harpoon him first, and once you have the croc on a rope you pull him to the surface and then shoot him. There were three of us in the canoe, Harry in the bow with the harpoon, me in the middle with the spotlight and rifle, and a bloke named Frank Mailgura paddling at the stern. So there was this croc sitting there, on the edge of the creek, in the water. We paddled gently, ever so quietly, towards him, for the slightest new sound would frighten him. The light seems to mesmerise them, and he didn't move.

Closer. Frank shook every drop off the paddle after each silent stroke. I had the light right on his head, and signalled to Frank how to approach the croc so Harry could get a sideways throw of the harpoon into its neck. Ten feet. The croc was a huge target, but Harry waited, ready. Six feet. Whack! The harpoon was in the croc's neck, the pole fell back into the water – we'd recover it later – and the croc dived, as we knew it would, but we had it on the rope. It was simply a matter of hauling it up gently, then shooting it. Frank was doing the right thing on the paddle, going backwards fast, so that we had the harpoon rope at the bow of the canoe. You can't see a thing in those muddy tidal creeks even in daytime, so it's essential to know, from the direction of the rope, that the crocodile is in front of the canoe not underneath it, especially when the croc is two feet longer than the canoe. But suddenly there was a tell-tale shaking of the root of one of the mangrove trees, which grow downwards like the tentacles on an octopus: uh-oh, the croc had tangled the rope around the root of a tree. So now all we knew was that the rope was tangled around the root and that somewhere down there, swimming free, was the crocodile. 'Oh well,' I thought, 'that's that, we'll cut the rope and go home. The harpoon head is just a couple of nails and the croc will get rid of it easily, but that's the end of this little adventure.'

So I thought. I grabbed a knife to cut the rope, but Harry said, 'Hang on, I'll get him' and he dived out of the canoe into the deep, milky water. I just couldn't believe it. Somewhere down there was a fourteen-foot-long croc, and Harry obviously intended to swim down, break off the root of the tree where it was tangled, and free the rope. We had no idea where Harry was: Frank was madly paddling the canoe in circles, and I was peering over the side of the canoe, vainly flashing the spotlight here, there, anywhere. Suddenly there was an almighty whack on the side of the canoe, behind me, and I thought I would die with fright. It's the croc, was my immediate thought, and I spun round to look. But no, there was the laughing face of H. Mulumbuk, Esquire, expert hunter, and he was holding – of all things – a bloody Log Cabin tobacco tin in his hand.

'I forgot my tobacco when I went in,' he said, passing it to me. 'Hang onto this, Ted.' And with that he dived under again. A minute later he surfaced again, having cleared the rope, and we proceeded to haul up the croc and shoot it. And then I sneaked a look inside Harry's precious – and I use the word advisedly – tobacco tin, and there inside were three bumpers and the tiniest little bit of tobacco, just enough for one 'long-pipe' full. He and Frank ritually filled the pipe, as they do in Arnhem Land, lit the tobacco, took a long heady pull each at the pipe, and then looked at me. I must have had the funniest look on my kisser, because they both started to roar with laughter. Then Harry said to me, 'Don't worry Ted. S'pose croc eat me, plenty more blackfellers.'

I contented myself with saying 'Bloody blackfellers, better off without them', and that really made them laugh.